# Taco Noir
## Tales of Culinary Crime

Steven Gomez

First Edition

Book Cover and design by Steven Gomez

Photography by Steven Gomez and Deborah Watson-Novacek

Printed in the USA

Noir Factory

www.noirfactory.com Copyright © 2012 Steven Gomez

All rights reserved.

ISBN: 0615635091
ISBN-13: 978-0615635095

Bon Appétit!

## DEDICATION

For Alfred Gomez

Who showed me which end of the spoon was which.

# CONTENTS

Acknowledgments i

Forward 1

The Case of the Vanishing Pits 5

The Case of the Upper Crust 15

The Case of the Unhappy Chickpea 27

The Case of the Second Story 38

The Case of the Hard-Boiled Monte Cristo 54

The Case of the Vintage Larceny 64

The Case of the Biting Spice 75

The Case of the Awkward High Note 91

The Case of the Fowl Prediction 109

The Case of the High Stakes 128

The Case of the Undercover Mulligan 142

The Case of the Absent Exhibit 160

Bonus Story! The Big Shoulders 172

# ACKNOWLEDGMENTS

First and foremost there is my wife, Deborah. Like most of what I do and who I am, this would not exist without her. From the big things to the small stuff, there is no way to list everything she does. I can only thank her for it.

Also there are my kids, Joseph and Kendall, who never fail to make me proud. My fondest wish is that they will be as proud of me as I am of them.

There is also my mother and my late father, to who this book is dedicated. They raised me on comic books, mysteries, and late-night horror films, and I learned these lessons well. A tip of the hat as well goes to my older siblings, Diana, Carol and Bea. They let me live.

I'm also indebted to one of my oldest and best friends, Alex Guilbert, for riding shotgun and feeding all interests noir, pulp, and comic.

And finally, a nod to Chris Anisko, another of my best and oldest friends, for being there whenever a plausible alibi was needed.

And for being the only guy I know with a gun.

## FORWARD

By Steven Gomez

There's a dark alleyway because there's always a dark alleyway. There's fog because there needs to be fog. There's a gin joint, a greasy diner, and a newsstand because it won't work if there isn't. In the distance a fog horn cries out, and the chill cuts its way through your coat like a rusty razor. You can see streetlights glow in the avenue beyond, but all they do is make the shadows that much darker. The smell of burnt coffee drifts through the air, and when the wind changes, so does the story.

It could be the Moroccan dive down the street, where the man at the bar sports a fez and peels fruit with a stiletto. It might be the hotdog cart up the road near where the cop patrols nightly and takes a piece of whatever action comes his way. It might even be the fresh-faced kid who slings hash at the local diner, who came to the big city to be a star but ended up in over her head.

There's a marriage between food and American detective fiction that is stronger than any other genre fiction. When we imagine the hero of a hard-boiled detective story, we rarely think of the detective in his office any longer than to pick up messages from his dedicated (and often leggy) secretary. When he visits his apartment long enough to hang up his fedora, it is usually empty with the exception of a rumpled bed and a cheap bottle of booze.

The detective's world is defined by the places people eat, drink, and congregate. Our hero crashes cocktail parties, meets informants at dive bars, and gets his heart started every morning in the local hash-house with coffee every bit as bitter as he.

From the lamb chops and sliced tomatoes of Sam Spade, the dry Martini of Nick Charles, Philip Marlow's bologna sandwiches, or Spenser's gourmet omelets, the food of the noir detective is every bit a staple of their world as is a snub-nose revolver. Bars, diners, and restaurants give the sleuth's world definition and, well… flavor. Without them, the black and white world of noir literature becomes exactly that.

The stories in this book all stem from a life-long love of great food and great detective stories. Some of the best times in my life have been defined by meals with friends, and stories shared. Going out to dinner with my parents as a kid meant going to a greasy spoon followed by a trip to the newsstand. A visit to grandma's house was heralded by the smell of percolated coffee and freshly-made tortillas. Diners, truck-stops, and dives made up an early part of my life just as bistros, tasting rooms, and cafes made up the later years. Put them together, and it's the best of both worlds.

I'd like to think that I am the first person to tie these genres together in this particular way, but I know I am mistaken. I've seen and appreciated mystery stories that have focused on regional foods and flavors, as well as included interesting recipes, but I think that this book is a singular sort of animal.

Our world-weary and slightly beaten no-name detective is driven not only by his search for a culinary excellence but also for justice. Although he is at times foolish, I've done my best (with the exception of the last story) to stay away from the ridiculous. Our hero is riddled with flaws and short-comings, but ennui isn't one of them. I'm a complete sucker for a bruised and battered hero who remains unbroken. Hopefully so are you.

The letter of the law is almost always broken and its spirit might suffer, but more often than not, justice is served. And it is usually served with the appropriate side dish.

# THE CASE OF THE VANISHING PITS

*When you deal with the mob, you gotta watch your stones*

Spring came late this year, fighting the good fight against the oppressive snow and the pelting rain that washed the city clean of its filth, if only for a moment. The sun visited as frequently as a paying client, but unlike those same clients, when it showed up it came like gangbusters. It beat through the clouds and filled the city with an unfamiliar sensation that I can only take as hope. For me, though, the bright sun cast long shadows into my life that brought me to mind of years past and of the Herm Walther case.

Herman was neither a good nor a kind man, which worked out well considering he was paid to be neither of those things. From the age of three he had a thirty-inch neck and an IQ to match. At age eight he probably shook down his first mark on the playground for his milk money, and developed a taste for it. With those skills well in tow, he left behind the confines of PS 102 and set out to make his way in the world. His way led him to the wrong side of the tracks.

Herm worked as hired muscle for a reptile by the name of Zack Demone. Demone was what we in polite society call a 'loan agent' and what made him a success in said field was the fact that he possessed an almost supernatural ability to find desperate mugs in need of a life line and bleed them dry. If further misfortune visited these suckers and they somehow fell behind in the payments on the soul-crushing interest that Zack charged, then he would compound said misery by visiting Herm on them. For having very little education, Herm Walther excelled in the field of payment restructuring.

It was on such a visit, while Herm was assisting a local merchant adjust his bottom line, that Herm was pinched by the cops. A quick glance into the holding cell that had seen plenty of Herm Walther in his thirty years of existence convinced the DA that Herm was an excellent candidate for an extended stay upstate. In Herm's chosen profession, a few years up the river was considered a hazard of the job, or even a mark of honor. Honor, like many other words, had no place in Herm Walther's vocabulary. Compound that with the fact that Herm's little woman was eight months pregnant at the time, Herm took his time in the holding cell to figure some new math. He sent word to the DA that there might be a deal to be made if some 'arithmetic' could be overlooked.

Working for years with Zack Demone had given Herm complete knowledge of his boss' dealings. It was perfectly understandable for Demone to assume that Herm Walther wasn't smart enough to notice his lips moving, let alone pay attention to Demone's dealings, but Walther was smarter than his boss gave him credit for. Not much, mind you, but just enough to be dangerous.

Walther's deal with the DA was for full immunity for any crimes committed while under Zack Demone's employment, both known and discovered under investigation. To Herm, it seemed like a sweet deal, one that would see him out of the clink by suppertime, and home for the spring to bounce little Herm Junior on his knee.

The only things that Herm had not been granted were protection and common sense.

On the day that Herm was to testify to the grand jury regarding Zack Demone's criminal activities, Herm was, for lack of a better term, 'absent.' Herm's absence had made as much impact as his presence did. The DA dropped the charges against Demone, and then proceeded to have a steak dinner, graciously provided by Demone. Demone himself had to go through the extensive interviewing process of hiring a new thug. The process took about five seconds. Nature, I'm told, abhors a vacuum, and the small one provided by Herm Walther's absence was soon filled, and the city went on its own merry, apathetic way.

With the exception of Mrs. Herm Walther and her new son, Herm Jr.

That's when yours truly fell into the picture. It had been my experience that lunks such as Herm Walther, for the most part, fell into relationships with women who were the female version of the same. Not that their knuckles dragged on the ground, you understand, but that they had similar compassions and sensibilities as the lugs they married. None-too-bright, as their mate, none-too-caring, and drifting along to wherever life might happen to deposit them. People like Herm Walther generally got what they asked for.

Not so with Mrs. Walther.

Elizabeth Walther washed up on my doorstep fresh-faced, eyes full of innocence and hope. And with a two month old boy in tow. Mrs. Walther was almost a baby herself, and what she knew of life could fill a matchbook. Once upon a time she had been told to be loving, honorable, and obedient, and had done her best to do all these things. Her husband had promised those things as well, but he also promised not to fink on his mobster boss, so it occurred to me that Herm Walther might have been a little light in the commitment department.

Elizabeth held out hopes for Herm's return, clearly the most optimistic individual I had ever met, and told me that the cops had not shared her sunny outlook. They dutifully took her statement and filed it in the trash when she wasn't looking. She had dragged Herm Jr. across the city looking for any clue to his Pa's whereabouts and had come up empty, but still determined. Her path, as well as her resources, had just about run dry, but if she could pay the rent with grit she would have lived in the Taj Mahal. She believed that her beloved Herm was still out there and she begged me to locate him.

Part of me wanted to tell her that she didn't so much need a private eye as a shovel, but one look into those wide, innocent baby-blues, and I couldn't refuse. She was a good kid, too good for the likes of Herm Walther, and if I could bring some closure to her then perhaps she could move on and give Herm Jr. the kind of life his old man never had.

Yeah, sometimes I'm stupid like that.

After Mrs. Walther left I placed a few phone calls, doing my best to stay off of Zack Demone's radar as I did so. Eventually an old pal of mine from the DA's office, Mike McCarthy, gave me the first lead I had. He confirmed that not only did the DA's case against Demone fall apart after Herm disappeared, but that he had been hearing rumors and whispers that Herm might have gone upstate after all, or as his informant had told him, "Herm had gone to live on the farm where his dog Rover lived."

McCarthy had assumed that his informant's wit was about as dry as Lake Erie, but I knew better. Word on the street was that Zack Demone had done all right by his mom when the big bucks began to roll in and bought her a spread out in the country that would turn Central Park a little greener with envy. Since it was out of character for Demone to do anything for anyone but himself, it was a good bet that this show of fondness for his old Ma had some kind of strings attached. We filled up on coffee and decided to take in the country air.

The farm itself was a slice of American Pie al a mode, a piece of Americana straight out of Ma and Pa Kettle. Despite all the down-home hokum, Mrs. Demone was a polite and civil hostess, and received us with old-world civility. She took us on a brief tour of the grounds, pointing out the fruit trees in the distance next to her victory garden. Sitting us down on the front porch, Ma Demone set Mike and me up with hulking pieces of homemade cherry pie and lemonade with the bite of a Doberman. The pie was the best I had ever eaten, and I told the old girl so. While we stuffed our pie holes with pie, Mrs. Demone talked our ears off about what a dream little Zackie was, and how busy he was making his fortune in the city. Ma Demone did say that even though Zack didn't spend much time visiting, he was thoughtful enough to send some of his 'little friends' to bring out the tree that had provided the very same fruit that she had used in the pie we were eating. They were even thoughtful enough to plant it for Mrs. Demone. In the middle of the night.

Mike and I suddenly got very full of pie.

While Mrs. Demone took our plates to the kitchen and went to refill our lemonade, Mike and I went out to the garden to have a closer look at the cherry tree. It was an impressive specimen among fruit trees, full of lush leaves and ripe cherries. The limbs were filthy with the fruit, even bowing with them, causing Mike and I to exchange concerned looks.

"That sure is one healthy tree," I told the copper.

"That it is," he agreed. "I bet she uses some powerful fertilizer."

We inspected the trunk of the tree and discovered that it had been planted fairly recently. When we got back to the porch, we thanked Mrs. Demone for the pie and the hospitality. The dear gave us each a peck on the cheek and wrapped up some fruit and sandwiches for the long ride back to the city. We left the farm and drove for about a mile and a half before Mike radioed the station and had the boys round up some shovels and a warrant and meet us at the Demone farm.

While we waited, Mike and I ate fruit and sandwiches.


The old girl was in all her glory, whirling this way and that as she filled glasses with lemonade and doled out sandwiches, pie and coffee. She was relishing every minute of our visit, and clearly seemed disappointed when the men finished their excavations and the coroner left for the city. As we watched Mrs. Demone clean up, I could only think of young Elizabeth Walther and the bitter pill I had for her and Herm Jr.

I knew that the young woman would take this hard, and I couldn't just go back to the girl empty handed. I closed my eyes and exhaled, looking to the untrained eye as if I might have been praying. I opened my eyes, and had no more inspiration than I had the moment before. I needed something to take some of the pain away.

And then it hit me....

# MA DEMONE'S SWEET CHERRY PIE

For the Crust (enough for top and bottom)

2 1/2 cups all-purpose flour

2 sticks unsalted butter

1 tsp. kosher salt

1 tsp. granulated sugar

8-9 tbsp. ice water or more if needed

For Filling

4 cups pitted fresh cherries (about 2 pounds unpitted)

4 tablespoons cornstarch

2/3 to 3/4 cup sugar (adjust this according to the sweetness of your cherries)

1/8 teaspoon salt

Juice of half a lemon

1/4 teaspoon vanilla extract

1 egg, beaten with 2 tablespoons water

- Preheat oven to 400 degrees F.

- Cut the butter into 1/2-inch cubes, put them on a baking sheet, and toss the sheet into the freezer for about an hour.

- In a mixing bowl, combine the flour, salt, and sugar and mix well. Slowly add the frozen butter cubes and cut them into the mixture using a pastry knife until you break up the butter to the size of large buckshot. Add the water slowly until the dough sticks to itself when you give it a pinch.

- Remove the dough from the bowl and put it onto a clean, dry, flat work surface. Press the dough into small discs. If the dough crumbles and doesn't cooperate, slowly add more water, tablespoon by tablespoon, until the dough shows you some respect.

- Sprinkle each disk lightly with flour and wrap individually in plastic wrap. Place in fridge for 1 hour.

- Stir the cherries, cornstarch, sugar, salt, lemon and vanilla extract together gently in a large bowl.

- Roll out half of the chilled dough on a floured work surface to a 13-inch round. Gently place the round into a 9-inch pie pan, either by rolling it around the rolling pin and unrolling it over the pan or by folding it into quarters and unfolding it in the pan. Trim edges to a half-inch overhang.

- Spoon filling into pie crust, discarding most of the liquid in the bowl.

- Roll out the remaining dough into a 12-inch round on a lightly floured surface, cover the filling, and trim it, leaving a 1-inch overhang. Fold the overhang under the bottom crust, pressing the edge to seal it, and crimp the edge nice and pretty, so as to make Ma Demone proud. Brush the egg wash over the pie crust.

- Cut slits in the crust with a sharp knife, forming vents, and bake the pie for 25 minutes. Reduce the temperature to 350 degrees F and bake the pie for 25 to 30 minutes more, or until the crust is golden. Let the pie cool on a rack.

Enjoy it with a nice, hearty cup of Joe.

# THE CASE OF THE UPPER CRUST

*More than just crust can be blown sky high.*

The noise coming from the doorman at Dino's Ristorante Italiano was a cross between a punch in the gut and the air slowly leaving a slashed car tire. Not that I would know firsthand. My friend smiled, taking the doorman's slack jaw and senseless stuttering as a referendum on her good looks and charming personality. While I generally agreed with such assessments, I had a feeling that the doorman's hesitation was due less to my captivating dinner guest's considerable charms and more to the fact that I had shown my persona in a place where I was considered mucho non grata. Muscling my way past the gaping jaws of the mute doorman, I opened the glass and mahogany door and escorted my guest inside.

It was still very early in the evening, well before the joint picked up a full head of steam, and there were only about a half-dozen souls in the place. The stiffs were busy making nice with each other, stuffing their faces, clinking their glasses, and chirping like well-fed birds. My companion and I made our way to the hat check girl. I removed my trench coat and she her stole, and we handed them forth. The girl, a red-headed gum chewer who I had seen the last time I was here, froze in mid-chew, her Juicy Fruit threatening to go overboard.

"It'll go stale that way," I said, using a couple of fingers to push the girl's yap shut. She remained still, but you could hear a gulping sound across the restaurant. The girl turned out to be solid after all, and rallied the troops enough to take our garments and stow them in the back, wherever overcoats go to sleep. My friend and I turned and walked towards the dining area, only to be stopped on the one yard line by a swarthy man-mountain in an industrial strength tuxedo.

"Youse aren't welcome here," said the monolith, a dark haired, mustached slab whose eyebrows met in the center of his forehead and embraced like old prep school chums.

"If I only went to places in town where I was welcome," I said, elbowing past the Cyclops on my way towards procuring a window table for my lovely companion and myself, "I would never go anywhere."

The man-mountain continued to stare, arms crossed over his chest and a look in his eye designed to instill terror in those who stood beneath his towering gaze. In my line of work, I had been intimidated by the best, so I held out a chair for my guest and took a seat for myself. The goon continued to stare us down, his eyebrows rising and falling with every breath, so I asked him for the wine list. He continued his stare until it dawned on him that his gaze was less-than-wilting, and he regained his ability to speak.

"Youse aren't welcome here," he repeated, the record apparently having a skip in that particular groove.

"We'll need to see a menu, of course," I told the troglodyte, "but go ahead and start us off with whatever passes for Chianti Classico in this joint."

A confused look passed over the big man's face, as if he were trying to divide one-thousand and eighty-three by fourteen. I imagine that he was debating whether or not he should throw us out on our keisters or if the rules had changed when he wasn't looking. Evidently uncertainty was on our side and the giant disappeared, reappearing moments later with a pair of glasses and a small jug of wine. He sat the glasses down and began to pour, only to freeze as an ear-splitting voice cut through the dining room.

"Luigi!" boomed the voice, causing the giant to snap the bottle upwards, a few stray drops of wine staining his lapel. The diners also stopped their revelry and turned their gaze to the kitchen, from where the voice issued. A man in a chef's toque and a white apron stood, butcher's knife in hand, glaring at my table. I took advantage of the lull to relieve the giant of his bottle and topped off our glasses.

The chef continued to stare until it dawned on him that he held the attention of every paying patron in the place. The sneer that decorated his face slowly and uncomfortably twisted into a clenched smile, one that bore only the faintest family resemblance to sincerity.

"Please, everyone, please! Eat! Drink! Be merry!" The chef lowered his knife as he walked towards our table, his free hand waving to regulars and greeting them, but his eyes never leaving us.

"Luigi," hissed the chef through his gritted teeth. "Get them the hell out of here!" Luigi snapped himself out of his stupor and put a firm hand on my shoulder, readying himself to make me his improvisational shot put. I countered his move with one of my own, shooting my hand into the left breast pocket of my jacket.

"Careful," I warned the two men. "You wouldn't want me to put a hole in my coat in the middle of your dining room, would you?"

Uncertainty washed over the big man, and he turned to the small chef for guidance. The chef's face flushed under the toque, and he gave a quick nod towards his large subordinate. Luigi took the cue, and his hand flew away from me as if I was the business end of an oscillating fan. I counted myself lucky that neither of them called my bluff, seeing as how I didn't have anything more lethal than old breath mints in my jacket. The chef's pinched smile held, and with a nod he sent the giant on his way, leaving the three of us at the table. With only two glasses between us, the cook was going to have to be the odd man out.

"What are you doing here?" hissed the chef, taking a seat and leaning forward conspiratorially. "You are no longer welcome here!"

"You told me that this was one of your favorite restaurants," teased my charming companion, sipping the Chianti through a smile.

"It is!" I protested. "Marco, tell the lady how much I love the menu here."

Marco shook his head at me and appeared to be on the verge of tears. Marco was the chef and owner of Dino's, the restaurant he had inherited from his father, who was named Gabe. As far as I could tell, the restaurant never even had a busboy named Dino let alone an owner.

"You promised me that you would never again come back here," whispered Marco, his eyes darting from table to table trying to identify the source of the icy shivers that made their way up his spine. Like any Ristorante worth its pasta, it was Saturday evening, and the place was filling up faster than a crooked charity Santa's pockets during the holiday shopping season. "You promised!"

"I did no such thing!" I corrected the sad little chef. "You made that assumption after you had me thrown out the last time I was here."

"Why would anyone do such a thing?" cooed my companion.

"Because," hissed the diminutive chef, "the last time he was here, three of my customers died."

"That's less than the time before that" I added to my friend. "Now that time was an event!"

Marco attempted speech, but the only thing that escaped him was a slight gurgling sound. Shifting his pleading gaze away from my less-than-sympathetic visage, he turned a desperate eye to my dinner guest, silently attempting to convince her to either charm me from his restaurant, or preferably, to bash me with the bottle of cheap Chianti on the table. I imagine that there was a small moment of hope when she picked up the bottle of wine.

"This is actually a quite decent bottle of Classico," my guest told him, eliciting yet another gurgle from the cook.

"This is the best pizza in the entire city," I told my friend. She waved a glass in Marco's direction in salute.

"Not true!" the chef protested. "Philippe's is better by far!"

"Nonsense," I corrected him. "Philippe's is strictly second fiddle to yours, my dear Marco." I looked back at my friend. "Marco does this thing with the crust that gives it a slight nutty flavor. Brilliance! Sheer Brilliance!"

"I can hardly wait," my companion said, shooting the chef a smile that would kill lesser mortals.

"Please," Marco beseeched us. "When you come here, it's only a matter of time till someone gets killed! I would prefer that it were not me!"

I took a sip of the Chianti and waited, watching the chef contort like a Wallenda. After a long ten count, I lowered my glass and looked the little man squarely in his beady little eyes.

"You know what I want," I said. He was shaking his head before I even finished my sentence.

"Forget it," he shot back at me. "I will never surrender that information to you!"

"In that case," I told Marco, picking up the small jug of wine and refilling my glass. "My friend and I will be forced to make dining here a habit." We raised our glasses and clicked them together. "What are your plans for tomorrow night?"

"Why I believe I am free," she answered, taking a lady-like slug of Chianti to seal the deal.

"Enough!" screamed Marco. He jumped from the table and stormed over to the bar where he grabbed a pad of paper from Luigi, who was busy pretending to stand upright. He picked up a pencil and scribbled furiously on the paper before tearing off the sheet and marching back to our table.

"Here!" Marco said, taking my hand and thrusting the wadded up paper into it. "Take this and may the devil take you as well! Now, a deal is a deal! Leave and never, ever return!"

I took a look at the paper and saw that it indeed held my prize. Folding the document carefully, I placed it into my breast pocket next to the breath mints, and stood up, pulling the chair out for my guest.

"Let's blow," I told her. "A deal is a deal."

"And what about diner?" she asked.

"Well," I said, taking her by the arm and leading her out amid the cowering glances of the wait staff. "I guess it's leftover meatloaf and mashed potatoes for us."

She sighed as we walked out the door and hailed a cab. I was fortunate. My companion had sampled my meatloaf and decided to come with me. I opened the cab door and we got in. She leaned over and whispered into my ear.

"What's on the paper?"

"It's Marco's recipe for pizza dough," I told her. "The recipe's been in the family for generations. At one time, the younger generation had to pay for the recipe in blood."

"Seriously?"

I raised an eyebrow. "No, not about the blood thing," she dismissed. "You really brought me all the way down here for a recipe?"

I was about to tell her that a family recipe was better than gold. It was like magic. If you had one as good as Marco's, you never, ever let the audience see what was behind the curtain. You simply let them experience the magic and take your bow. I could have offered Marco money for the recipe, but he never would have gone for it. That crust was the stuff that dreams were made of, so in order to get a slice I had to apply what leverage I had. I would have told her all that, but she cut me off.

"Why don't we go to your place and you can whip up some pizza for us?"

It didn't work that way. In order for the magic trick to work right, you had to set it up. Like all the good things in life, anticipation was the key.

The cab pulled away and all conversation died as a giant blast erupted, tearing through the night and sending the cab spinning out of control. A hail of glass and pebbles rained down on the auto, and it skidded to a stop on the curb across the street from Dino's Ristorante Italiano.

Or what used to be Dino's Ristorante Italiano.

"What was that?" my lady friend gasped. She struggled to right herself in back as the cabbie shook off the effects of the blast.

"From the sound of it, I'd say about eight sticks of dynamite." I pinched my nose and blew, trying in vain to chase away the ringing in my ears. Whoever put the dynamite in Dino's was a rookie. It was an old building. Eight sticks were probably overkill. So to speak.

"Marco was right," gasped my friend. "People do die around you."

"Nonsense," I told her. "People die because there is a certain subspecies that do things like lie, cheat, bomb buildings and shoot their fellow human beings. They are the reason that things fall over and people die. I'm just the guy who is trying to make some pizza."

I told the cabbie to take us to my apartment, but my companion begged off, mumbling something about self-preservation as she did. I sighed and took notice of the dark plume of smoke coming from the ruins behind us. I had my prize, but a good crust was only part of the magic trick. It seemed if I wanted the whole act, I'd have to come up with a sauce recipe of my own.

# MARCO'S MAGIC PIZZA CRUST

2 ½ cups whole flour (separated)

1 cup lukewarm water

2 ¼ teaspoons instant yeast

1 teaspoon salt

2 teaspoons olive oil

- Take a small bowl and knock out about a half cup of the flour, the water, and the yeast. Mix it around until it looks like yeast soup and cover with plastic wrap. Put it aside for about ten minutes or so, or approximately two or three chapters of a Mickey Spillane novel.

- When you get back to the soup, things should be happening. The yeast should be hard at work making a wet, spongy mass. In a mixing bowl, pour in the remaining flour and mix the salt into the flour. Pour in your yeast soup and top it off with the olive oil. Mix it all up until it is well incorporated, and then dump the whole caboodle onto a well-floured surface and give it the third degree.

- Don't be too gentle with the mess. Knead the dough until it takes on a smooth consistency, just the opposite of what you would look like under similar circumstances. Cover the larger bowl with plastic wrap and let it live in your refrigerator for a day or two.

That's right. A day or two.

- The next day (or so) pull out the dough a couple of hours before you use it. It should be fatter than a bookie's wallet after the Derby. Give it an hour or so to come to room temperature, and then punch the sucker in the mug. This lets out the gasses the yeast creates and gives you a satisfied feeling deep down in what passes for your soul. Preheat the oven for about an hour at 450 degrees F, and if you have a pizza stone, well la-de-da.

- On a floured surface, stretch or roll the dough out to a thin, circular size, about sixteen inches in diameter, or whatever will fit on your pizza stone or cookie sheet. If you are using a pizza stone, put the crust on a peel that has been liberally dusted with cornmeal. If you are putting the dough on a cookie sheet, for the love of Pete please put some parchment paper down or something. After all, are we not civilized?

- Top the crust with your favorite sauce, a goodly amount of cheese, and whatever toppings tickle your fancy. Paint what's left of the crust (the mythical Cornicione) with a little of the left over sauce. Gently place your creation into the oven for ten minutes, and remove carefully.

- When your pie is out, let it rest for ten minutes and enjoy. Now, you might be tempted to cut down on some of the wait time on the first part of the recipe. Don't do it! Remember, men have died for this.

# THE CASE OF THE UNHAPPY CHICKPEA
*When life deals you falafels, make a pita.*

I n my line of work, it helps if you can keep your eyes open and your ear to the ground, or something like that. You make friends, or what passes for friends, with everyone from mob men to choir boys, hoping that they'll feed you whatever scraps of info you need to get by. I do my best to keep ahead of the comings and the goings around this burg, hoping that when things break my way it results in a payday. The first rule of business is that if you stand in line waiting for clients to come to you, more often than not you go hungry. Today I was in pursuit of both knowledge and lunch, and Lady Luck was my dining partner.

"The McDermott's were in court this morning," Manny told me as he handed me a steaming hot falafel pita wrapped up in yesterday's newsprint. Manny runs the falafel wagon outside of the city courthouse, and was as permanent a fixture there as a hotdog cart at a Saturday baseball game or a gang boss at Sunday service. Everyone from Superior Court Justices to the court stenographers made at least one meal a week from Manny's cart, and because of that Manny was a fixture at the court. He knew every case that was open in every courtroom in the building, and every Joe that set foot inside. Manny was so much an everyday part of courthouse life that the only way you would notice him would be when he wasn't there.

Manny was never not there.

"The McDermotts," I mumbled through a mouthful of deep-fried heaven. Manny, to his credit, was fluent in the language of gluttony and had no problem keeping up. "I hear that they're pretty big money."

"The biggest," Manny said, handing me a much needed napkin. I took it because I figured I would end up wearing more of the falafel than eating it, and noticed that Manny kept his hand stretched out. Forgetting to collect payment for a sandwich is not how a guy like Manny kept his spot front-and-center at the courthouse since Moses was in diapers. I fished into my anemic-looking wallet and handed the street gourmand a sawbuck. He slipped the dirty, wrinkled bill into his pocket and didn't bother coming back to me with any change.

I first made the cook's acquaintance about a dozen years ago or so. He had already been at his spot long enough to attract dust, but a new operator in the area had tried to squeeze Manny for protection. When you make a steady paycheck in this burg, there's always a new operator who wants a taste. Manny employed yours truly to have a small chat with said operator, and I came out on top. In return, Manny kept me in falafels and hummus for a whole year, but the meter had expired on our arrangement long ago. I took his the absence of change on his part to mean that he had a tip, rather than assume he now served the most expensive sandwiches on the planet.

"All right," I said as I fished around for another napkin to help eradicate the evidence of a deep fried lunch from my trench coat. "Spill!"

"The McDermotts are in the middle of a particularly ugly divorce," Manny said, dicing an onion as he spoke. "They're pointing fingers at each other, accusing the other of sleeping around."

"That's how they play the game, isn't it?" I asked, still wiping my fingers. Manny was a master of oil, hot sauce, and tahini, and while his cart might not be much to look at, what he did there was so good it should have been illegal in most states. "Each side tells the judge that the other side done them wrong, they slide hizhonor a fat envelope, and the fattest envelope wins."

From what I knew about Little Anthony McDermott, I felt it would have been a safe bet to assume that his envelope was the fattest. He owned all the radio stations in town and about half of the movie houses. He made his money the old-fashioned way, through dead relatives, and from what Manny told me, he would spend more cash betting on an afternoon game between the Yankees and the Red Sox than he would like to see doled out to the little woman. Apparently Little Anthony held big grudges.

"In this case, all bets are off," smiled Manny. "Their case ended up in Judge Thurston's courtroom."

I stopped my post-sandwich wipe down long enough to digest this little tidbit along with my high calorie lunch.

Judge Lawrence Thurston was the last of the hard cases, and in a city where most of the judges wore parking meters around their necks, he was as solid as oak. He couldn't be bought, influenced, or threatened, and he absolutely despised mouths with silver spoons in them. It served McDermott right. The only reason he ended up in Thurston's court was because he was apparently too naïve or cheap to bribe the docket clerk to put his case in the hands of a judge who could be bought.

"Thurston, huh?" I replied. "I guess that there IS a chance that Mrs. McDermott might get what's coming to her."

"Not if Little Anthony has any say in the matter."

"What do you mean?" I asked. "There's no way that Thurston would let this case get bounced to another courtroom." Once the judge had a case, he was like a dog with a soup bone.

"I heard Little Anthony talking to his mouthpiece," Manny said, glancing over his shoulder for any passers-by of the non-customer type. "He told his lawyer to get some shamus on the job to dig up some dirt on his wife. Something that he can beat her over the head with in court, so to speak."

"And said mouthpiece hasn't yet found said shamus to dig up said dirt?" I asked, figuring that Manny had earned his change from the sawbuck.

"One can only assume," said Manny, turning his considerable talents to a bin full of chickpeas. "One can only assume."

I caught up with Little Anthony McDermott as he was exiting the courtroom. He was shooting daggers at the Mrs. and her meek little mouse of an attorney. Mrs. McDermott, a striking blonde in her late thirties, seemed immune to Little Anthony's considerable charm, probably from years of waking up to that same enduring sneer. Her mouth-piece, though, looked as rattled as a can of salted peanuts.

"Do the world a favor, Anthony," shouted the Mrs. across the bow of her lawyer. "Drop dead."

"Oh, it won't be me who's doing the dropping, peaches," called back Little Anthony, stepping towards the little woman. His lawyer, a much more seasoned and substantial mouthpiece, stepped between McDermott and the object of his affections, pushing back his client before he could do anything hasty in a courthouse lobby full of witnesses.

"Keep your head on, Mr. McDermott," said the suit, a guy in his fifties with salt and pepper hair and a mustache that made him look as if he tied young women to railroad tracks and laughed maniacally in his spare time. "We've got to play this one by the book. Judge Thurston will be all over you until this is through."

"I'm cool, I'm cool!" snapped Little Anthony, stopping in his tracks and straightening his suit. He gave the Mrs. one last sneer as she blew him a raspberry on her way out. I guess the spark wasn't completely gone.

I took this moment to walk towards McDermott so that I could introduce myself and offer my humble services. Mrs. McDermott was a pistol, and he was a keg of dynamite, so it was only a matter of time till one of them did something stupid. In his case, he could afford to pay for court-documented photos of his wife caught in the act of "stupid." I stepped in front of the bulldog of a man, relying on my bulk to stop him. He was in such a hurry to get out of the courthouse he almost bowled me over instead.

"Watch where you're going, flat foot," barked Little Anthony as he tried to elbow past me. I gave him a quick bow and my best soft-soap salesman voice.

"I'm no copper, Mr. McDermott," I told the little bulldog, looking down into his eyes. I told him my name, and mentioned that I was in the investigations racket. "The word around the old courthouse is that you are in need of someone with my particular … skill set."

"Standing in my way?" he snapped. I considered telling him he might need someone to help him reach the top of his bookshelf, but reminded myself that I was trying to pick up a client as opposed to losing one.

"I believe that he may indeed be of some use to us, after all, Mr. McDermott," said his slick lawyer. I smiled a little wider at the two, hoping that action wouldn't result in a case of diabetes.

"Oh," replied Anthony dumbly to his mouthpiece. Time seemed to stand still as Little Anthony took this simple concept and rolled it over in his mind. "You mean he can get the goods on Martha and we can turn it over to Judge Tightwads in there." Eureka. Apparently Little Anthony could put two and two together and occasionally come up with four. He was truly a testament to private education.

"Uh…not how I would put it, but yes," agreed the shyster. If Little Anthony McDermott ever heard the phrase "no," it certainly wouldn't have come from this mug.

"Fine," said McDermott, turning away once again and aiming his fire plug body towards the front entrance. "Get me some pictures, something I can use in court, and I'll toss a little something your way." He got to the door and paused, looking annoyed at his mouthpiece. The lawyer scrambled to open the door for his pugnacious client. "Heck, I might even give you a sawbuck or two."

I had paid a sawbuck for the falafel and the tip on the McDermott case, and an extra sawbuck wasn't even worth my conversation with Little Anthony. If Anthony was empathetic enough to tell my feelings, or anyone's feelings, he didn't let on. I was about to tell the little man where he could place his sawbuck when his lawyer stepped between us, having the good sense that he should earn his retainer. Before the shyster or I could tell Anthony anything, the taxi containing the little woman and her lawyer drove past. Little Anthony filled the air with a tirade of obscenities that would offend a sailor's delicate sensibilities.

I let the lawyer and Anthony go, following them out of the building. The attorney hailed a cab while a limo pulled up for Little Anthony. As the lawyer climbed into the cab to leave, I wondered why he wasn't leaving with McDermott. Looking into the limo, I got my answer.

The windows of the limo were covered, unlawful as hell, but when you have money, the world is the oyster you shuck. Little Anthony closed the door and the car sped away, but before it did I caught a glimpse of a well-manicured hand resting on McDermott's leg. It was dripping with expensive jewelry, and between that and the rubbing motion it was performing on Little Anthony's leg, I assumed that it wasn't his kid sister. I watched the tail lights of the limo fade into the night before walking back to Manny's falafel cart.

I reached into the tub of ice that Manny kept next to his cart and pulled out a bottle of pop. I rested the bottle top on the edge of Manny's cart and gave it a smack, shooting the cap into the air and earning a look of irritation from Manny.

"'It'll be a nickel for the pop," Manny growled.

"Take it out of that sawbuck I gave you earlier," I said, draining the bottle and debating whether to give the bottle back to the sandwich man or keep it for the deposit. "The McDermott case dried up." I told him about Little Anthony's inclination for thrift in matters of the heart, and looking at the pop bottle, Manny mentioned that there was a lot of that going around. I tossed the pop bottle over to him.

"You're aware that it takes two to tango?" asked Manny, an impish grin spreading across his mug. It took me a moment, but the impish grin crossed my face as well.

I thought of the well-manicured, bejeweled hand giving McDermott's leg a pat down earlier, and it occurred to me that if Mr. McDermott wasn't going to pony up the cash to seal up his divorce case, then the soon-to-be former Mrs. McDermott and her lawyer might. I bid Manny a good evening and turned towards the street to get a cab of my own when Manny called after me.

"It's STILL a nickel for the pop," he said. I flipped a silver dollar over my shoulder, and never heard it hit the sidewalk.

"Keep the change," I told him. I heard the dollar clink as it went into his change purse.

"What change?" he laughed as he started dicing up the chickpeas for the night court session.

# MANNY'S COURT HOUSE FALAFEL

2 cups dried chickpeas, sorted and rinsed

1 teaspoon baking powder

¼ cup chopped cilantro

Pinch of salt

1 onion, chopped

4 cloves of garlic, crushed

1 tablespoon ground cumin

1 tablespoon ground coriander

½ teaspoon red pepper flakes

¼ cup chopped parsley

Pepper

Oil for frying

8 warmed pitas

Tahini sauce

- Dump the chickpeas in a bowl and drown them in water overnight. Next drain the little suckers and give them a quick rinse. Toss the peas into a processor and grind them until they are chopped like a hot car. Throw in the baking powder, onion, garlic, and the dry ingredients. Pulse the mix until it can't be pulsed no more and season with the salt and pepper.

- Pour the oil in a pan and crank up the heat until it gets to 375 degrees F.

- Roll the falafel mixture like a juvenile delinquent rolls a tourist. If you are like the delinquents I know, you should have a bunch of two-inch, Ping-Pong-sized balls. Fry the balls in the hot oil, turning them until they are a light, crusty, dark brown on all sides. Remove them and drain them on a paper towel-lined plate.

- Drop the falafel balls onto a warm pita and drizzle a little of the tahini sauce over it. Top your pita with a little cheese and some shredded lettuce. Or don't. What do I care?

If you don't have any tahini sauce, here's a trick a mug in Casablanca taught me. Take a ½ cup of tahini (and by that I mean sesame seed paste), add three cloves of crushed garlic, ½ teaspoon of salt, three tablespoons of olive oil, ¼ cup of lemon juice, and a small bunch of parsley. Dump them into a food processor, give them a whirl, and whip 'em like they were cheating at cards.

# THE CASE OF THE SECOND STORY EXPOSURE

*Where what's good for the soul is good for the gander*

I stumbled into my office on a miserable, dank January morning. I had spent the entire week in the woods tailing an unfaithful husband and it had rained the entire time, leading me to believe that God doesn't much care for me. What had started as a case of the sniffles had picked up steam and turned into a full-blown case of evil. I plopped down on my office couch and watched the ceiling fan spin. Five minutes later I realized that my fan wasn't on, so I closed my eyes and tried to get some rest.

I came to the office to get some rest because the postage stamp I call an apartment has a cot in it that saw double-duty at Valley Forge, and I know from past experience that the couch in my office is the most comfortable piece of furniture I own.

Don't ask.

After a while I drifted in and out of consciousness, with visions of my past coming back to haunt me like Ebenezer Scrooge on a holiday bender. I woke up to a machine gun sneezing fit. After the last of the sneezes faded, I heard a familiar voice say "Gesundheit."

I sprang up from my couch, and then immediately regretted it. The ceiling fan was now still, but the rest of the room spun counter clockwise. Little red dots clouded my vision and when I connected them they spelled out expletives. I melted back down into my couch

"Jimmy Two-Fingers," I sighed, lying back onto my sickbed. "How did you get in here? I could have sworn I had locked the door?" I could have been mistaken. In the state I was in, I was lucky I was in the right office.

"You did, but what's a little breaking and entering between old pals," the reprobate asked. Jimmy Two-Fingers was a short, wiry little second-story man I knew from the neighborhood. I had known Jimmy for most of my life, back even when he was known as Jimmy Four-Fingers. He was a quick, graceful man who could make his way into a penthouse, clean the place out, and have a credible alibi before you knew you were missing Granny's china.

I reached towards a nearby lamp to turn it on, but Jimmy grabbed my arm before I could pull the cord. The effort took it out of me, so once again I renewed my close acquaintanceship with the couch.

"Ixnay on the amplay," said the burglar. He was fluent in Pig Latin. "I'm in the soup right now, and I need to be discreet." It was news to me that Jimmy knew words like 'discreet.'

"Jimmy, I don't suppose that you took the locked door as a sign that I wasn't entertaining?" I groaned.

"If you didn't want to entertain no visitors," answered Jimmy with a grin, "then you should get a better lock than that piece of cake you got on your door."

It was a valid point, and my gun wasn't handy, so I conceded it. I watched as Jimmy found the seat that I usually reserve for the paying clientele and made himself at home. He took out a cigarette, lit it with a small chrome flip-top, and flicked it closed with one hand, which is no small feat when your nickname is "Two-Fingers."

"It all started when I did a B&E for Big Tommy Markowitz over on the West End," said Jimmy, settling in to the tale as if he were reading a tyke "The Three Bears."

"And when did you start working for Big Tommy?" I asked. "The last I heard, you were strictly small time."

"Thanks," said Jimmy, blowing smoke in my face. "I appreciate that." I waved the puff of noxious fumes and told him to continue. "Big Tommy calls me up when he needs certain items… liberated from people who might have him in a compromising position."

"Oh dear lord," I gasped, and tried to sit up. The congestion in my head told me otherwise, so we compromised and I raised my head slightly. "Tell me that you aren't blackmailing Big Tommy Markowitz!"

"I happen to be quite fond of my remaining fingers," said Jimmy dryly. "I staked out the apartment of a small time operator who at this moment," Jimmy rolled back a sleeve and checked his watch, "well, I'd avoid the fresh fish for a while if I were you."

"Sounds charming," I said, my voice sounding as if it I had a bucket on my head. "Where do I come in?"

"Well, as I retrieved the items for Big Tommy, I couldn't help but notice that there were other subjects that had captured the artist's eye."

"Don't tell me," I barked, my voice once again interrupted by rapid-fire coughing. I recovered my voice but not my common sense. "You helped yourself to a fistful of blackmail photos."

"I helped myself to some photos that would have done no one any good, now that the photographer was...?"

"Chum?" I suggested.

"Indisposed," he offered. "Anyway, I couldn't just let all those compromising pics just fall into the hands of some cleaning lady...."

"Or police officer?" I asked.

"Like the cops wouldn't put the finger on some schmo stepping out on his Mrs." said Jimmy. I'd had run-ins with some of the beat cops in the city, and I had to agree that Two-Fingers had a point. "I performed a public service and burnt the pictures."

"All the pictures?" I asked.

"Well... most of the pictures," Jimmy offered. I had a bad feeling that this was where yours truly fell into the picture. "Not everybody involved in this little blackmail scheme was exactly pure as the driven snow. I had a chance to flip through the photos and I found this little gem."

Jimmy passed me a picture and I did my best to reach for it. Kind soul that he was, Jimmy walked over to me and held it while my hands tried to catch up. I took the picture, and when it was done spinning, I was able to make out two faces, a man and a woman, in a passionate embrace. With all the leaves and vines in the foreground of the picture, it was easy to surmise two things.

One was that the photographer was a scumbag who made his way sandbagging people when they were at their most vulnerable. Whatever was happening to the parasite at the hands of Big Tommy Markowitz, while unpleasant, was richly deserved.

The other thing that jumped out at me was the mugs captured in mid-embrace. The woman's face was well known to anyone who picked up a newspaper in the city, and not just on the society page. That woman was Ellie Danforth, and Ellie was a part-time saint and full-time fund raiser. She helped fund everything from hospitals, boy scouts, orphans, strays, and the occasional nun. She was widely regarded as the Florence Nightingale of a city that was woefully short on Florence Nightingales. But the picture also showed that Ellie Danforth had an Achilles' heel. The man in the photo wasn't Ellie's husband. It turned out that the saint was just as human as the rest of us.

"So what do you want to do with this?" I asked Two-Fingers. In all the time I had known Jimmy, he had strictly been a second story man. In his line of work, he had the opportunity to run numbers, even a protection racket or two. Lots of things that would be easier on a man missing more fingers than he possessed, but Jimmy always passed them up. Now the opportunity of the big payday had come, and I was curious as to which of his angels the old burglar would listen to.

"From what I gathered, the scumbag who took these already had their hand in Mrs. Danforth's pocketbook," said Jimmy, looking as my carpeting as if the threadbare rug would come together and spell out the answer to him. Without looking up, it seemed as if the carpet gave him what he was looking for.

"She needs to know that she ain't under this guy's thumb anymore," he said. "She needs to get this back."

"Well, good luck getting it back to her," I said. "Don't let the door smack you on the keister on the way out."

"Wattaya mean?" he asked. I guess that the rug had dummied up on him. "I did my part. Didn't you see me have my moment just then? I gave the pics to you, and now you gotta get 'em to her."

I sighed as a rattling sound made its way through my chest and worked its way into a coughing fit. I closed my eyes and worked my way through it, and when I opened my eyes, Jimmy Two-Fingers was gone and I had a case.

During the last few years I had cultivated a long list of sources and informants, most of it through favors, intimidation, and good-old fashioned threats. In the past I had been able to track down fences, number runners, enforcers, and even the odd hit-man or two. When it came to tracking down saints, however, that was where the system hit a snag.

What I learned through my sources was that Ellie Danforth didn't make bets with any of the bookies in the city, hadn't tried to have anyone bumped off, wasn't in the market to buy or sell hot merchandise, and wasn't looking for any narcotics.

Sometimes when the pigeon I'm looking for has a taste for the finer things, I can take a peek at the society pages or lay a saw-buck across the palm of a greedy doorman or a desperate waiter. Even a tailor or jeweler could provide me with a something, but this case was going nowhere. People in my line just didn't know how to work with a "decent" human being.

For those cases, we usually just drank.

The park across the street from the Danforth residence was the pride of the city, and unlike the parks on my side of town, they actually had cops who patrolled the neighborhood. My head still pounded to beat the band and I was running a temperature, but I kept an eye on the mansion across the road. I also got run off so many times I was beginning to develop a case of athlete's foot. Somewhere in my comings and goings the Danforths went on their merry way, and it took me three days before I got a solid bead on Little Ellie Danforth.

It turned out that Ellie volunteered time at the Sisters of Mercy, a hospital on the East Side, my neck of the woods and about a block from my office. I didn't beat myself up too much over this. Whatever went on inside the minds of saints and do-gooders was foreign land.

The lobby inside the Sisters of Mercy was worn, beat, and would have lost in comparison with any hospital outside of a war zone. The line waiting for care was significant in both length and despair. The nurse behind the desk looked as if she had experienced her fair share of misery as well, and when it came to my turn in line, she never bothered to look up.

"Uh…hello," I said, channeling my inner Cary Grant. I eventually got the old maid to abandon her interest in the comics section and look up at me, my toothiest grin on display. I managed to turn her frown, but it became a sneer rather than a smile.

"Take a number," she barked, pointing towards a wheel that one tends to find in your finer delis. I looked around the waiting room and decided that I might in fact be the sickest person in the group, so I did. I waited for the nurse to call my number and, as I did, reluctantly made small talk with a codger who parked himself next to me. For a while he droned on about hemorrhoids, arthritis, and gout, and I silently prayed for my ears to congest as much as my nose. Eventually a candy striper stopped by and dropped off some magazines for the room. The old guy pounced on them like a cougar on venison, and when I reached for one of the magazines for myself, I got the stink-eye from the old coot.

"I'll be done in a minute," he squawked, and I pulled back my hand before any of the fingers went missing. Taking pity on me, the young candy-striper gave me a copy of the morning edition.

"This should hold you over for a while," she said. "The doctor should see you shortly."

I started to say thank-you to the young woman with the sing-song voice as I took a look at the young biscuit for the first time. She was an angel with raven hair, alabaster skin, and the rosy complexion of someone who didn't spend their evenings in parks staking out do-gooder heiresses.

I'd seen the candy-striper before, and the pictures didn't do her justice. She was Ellie Danforth.

"Mrs. Danforth?" I croaked, my question fading into a series of coughs and sputters.

"Why…yes," answered Ellie, her angelic smile giving way to confusion as to how this scruffy stranger knew her name.

"Mrs. Danforth," I sputtered, trying to catch my breath. I reached into the breast pocket of my jacket for the envelope that Jimmy Two-Fingers had provided me. "I have some pictures that were taken of you that you might be interested in."

I don't know what reaction I was expecting, but I wasn't prepared for what I got. A quick shot to the chin proved to yours truly that just because a dame had been brought up in charm school didn't mean that she couldn't put a little shoulder behind a punch.

"You creep!" spat Ellie, her angelic face contorting to demonic. "I can't believe that scum like you could be a brazen as to walk right into the Sisters of Mercy and try to put the touch on me!"

"No, wait," I stammered, the pain in my head now fighting it out with the pain in my jaw. "You got it all wrong!"

"Billy! Tim!" she yelled into the nearby hallway. As if by magic two slabs of meat dressed in orderly's whites appeared, and they didn't seem to be the nurturing sort.

"Is this guy botherin' you, Ellie?" said one of the slabs.

"This …gentleman needs to be escorted off the grounds," said Ellie, her jaw as clenched as mine now was. "And you needn't be delicate about it."

I started to protest, but neither Tim nor Billy seemed to be open to debate. Working much faster than I would have thought men so large could work, Tim had one of my arms bent behind me and his free hand around my neck while Billy picked up my legs. Or maybe it was the other way around. Regardless of the order, the effect was the same. I was "escorted" to the side entrance where I was ejected from the Sisters of Mercy with particular care given to distance and propulsion.

I spent a few moments doing an inventory of the parts of my body that hurt, but gave up when I made it to the ache in my head. The unfortunate part of being thrown out of a hospital is that when it occurs, you are most likely to need one.

I sat down on the bench outside the hospital and planned my next move. The most prudent seemed to be going home, having a shot, hitting the hay, and then finding Jimmy Two-Fingers and smacking him about the head and upper torso. I suppose there must have been some comfort in the thought, because my eyelids fell like the stock market, and I drifted off to sleep.

"Excuse me?" said a voice, accompanied by a gentle nudge. I had fallen asleep on the bench, and rolled over onto my side. "Are you all right? Do you have a place to sleep?" It was a familiar voice in a tone much more pleasant than I had previously heard.

"Mrs. Danforth!" I gasped, turning over to face the young lady. Once again, her features changed from saintly to down-right homicidal.

"Oh, it's you again," she spat, backing up and looking around for what I assume was more simian orderlies. She had a small thermos in her hand, and I thought she was going to brain me with it as she turned.

"Wait, please," I said, sitting up. "I'm not the mug who's been trying to lean on you. I've been given these pictures and instructed to tell you that you don't have anything to worry about. Your blackmailer is out of the picture."

Words failed Mrs. Danforth as she opened the envelope and peeked inside. Almost dropping her thermos she quickly stashed the pics in her coat and pulled it closed as if they were gold.

"Is this on the level?" Ellie asked.

"Scout's honor," I said, getting to my feet before falling back to the bench. A salute was still a little too much for me. "A friend asked me to make sure you knew that you were out of the woods."

"Oh thank you!" said Ellie, wrapping her arms around me and hugging me tightly. I felt the air rush from my lungs as the thermos dug into me and I wondered how a society dame had developed such strength. She quickly composed herself and straightened up as I got to my feet.

"S'okay," I mumbled as thoughts of a warm bed filled my head. "You have a good life."

"I will!" she said, her face once again the beaming, angelic vision that Jimmy had imagined. She waved good-bye and I turned to head homeward. As I did so, Ellie called after me.

"What caused the blackmailer's sudden change of heart?" she asked, doubt once again crossing her saintly visage. "Did he come to some harm?"

"Not at all," I told the angel. "He's gone to live on a farm upstate where he has plenty of room to run and play."

"Oh good," she said, turning to walk towards the Sisters of Mercy. "It's nice when things turn out well."

"It sure is," I said as I started back to the office where I could lie down with some blankets and a hot water bottle. I only got a few steps before I heard a voice call after me. I turned and it was the angel. She ran to me, and I stood there stupid as she did. When she reached me she planted one on my cheek that would have made a statue blush, and I felt her press something into my hands. She smiled and left me in the cold, dark night.

Looking down, I found the small thermos the angel carried thrust in to my hand. Inside I found what might have been just the thing to chase away my cold, if not turn me into a good man.

And I wasn't splitting it with Jimmy.

# ANGELIC CHICKEN SOUP

1 medium chicken

1 large onion

3 sprigs of dill, tied into a bouquet

4 stalks of celery, chopped

3 cloves of garlic

3 tablespoons chopped ginger

1 turnip, cubed into 1/2-inch pieces

3 medium carrots, peeled and cut into 3-inch pieces

Juice of 1 lemon

2 tablespoons salt

2 potatoes, cubed into 1 inch pieces

1/2 cup matzo meal

2 large eggs room temperature, beaten

2 tablespoons vegetable oil

2 tablespoons seltzer water

1 teaspoon salt

1/2 teaspoon pepper

1 teaspoon finely chopped fresh dill

- Take the bird with a little bit of reverence and a little bit of trepidation and give her a quick wash. Toss her into the pot and keep her company with the onion, dill, celery, and salt. Turn up the heat on the fowl and sweat her to a boil. Keep up the heat and skim the foam off the top as you go. Once your bird is good and boiling, lower the heat to medium and toss in the ginger, turnip, carrots, and lemon juice. Cover and cook on low until the bird has served her two hour sentence.

- Season the bird to taste. The chicken should be nice and tender and ready to fall apart. Let the bird cool and carve the meat off of the carcass. Toss half of the meat back into the pot and put the rest on ice for another day. Crank up the heat on the pot and toss in the potatoes. Once you get the fowl simmering again, you're ready for the matzo balls.

- Toss the matzo meal, eggs, oil, seltzer, salt and pepper into a bowl and work them over. Put them on ice and let them chill for about a half hour. Once the mix is nice and cold, take it out and, with wet hands, work over the matzo with a pugilistic fervor and form the mess into 1 inch rocks. Drop the matzo balls into the soup and cover. Continue to simmer the soup for a half hour longer. Trust me, good things will happen.

- Spoon the soup into bowls and serve. Garnish with a dollop of sour cream or green onions. Or don't. Either way it's wellness in a bowl.

Serves 8, unless they're greedy.

# THE CASE OF THE HARD-BOILED MONTE CRISTO
*Sometimes you can Count more than just cards*

In this city, gambling is the organ grinder that makes the monkey dance. On the one hand, it is the topic of lectures, debates, and sermons. It gives politicians a target to shoot their intellectual water pistols at. It gives the copy editors something splashy to put on the front page above the fold. It also gives the good people of Hicksville something to raise their torches and pitchforks against.

If you dig a little deeper into the city's seamier side, you'll also find that gambling helps fund some of the soup kitchens in the lower East side, pays for the trash pick-ups at City Hall, and helps line the bottom of the collection plate at St. Dominic's Cathedral every Sunday.

Don't get me wrong. I'm no preacher from the church of the natural seven. At the same time gambling was bringing fortune and notoriety to a city growing in leaps and bounds, it was also responsible for little Joey going homeless because dear old dad put the deed to the house on a "sure thing." It cost many a sweet young thing their diamond rings because their sugar daddies couldn't cover the action that they asked for. And it also sent any number of schmucks to the bottom of the river because their mouths were bigger than their wallets. In fact, it seemed like some days there just wasn't enough river to cover them all.

It was a sad story, but none of that mattered to me. I was holding kings over aces.

"It's your bet," said Sweet Jesse Vasquez, the man hosting this evening's festivities. Sweet Jesse was a short, bald, round man who spent his life mopping up the rivers of sweat that made their way down his forehead. In order to keep that kind of hydration flowing, Jesse kept a personal pitcher of water and a glass nearby. The man could sweat in a snowstorm, earning him the unfortunate and completely behind-his-back nickname of "Sweat Jesse Vasquez." As my papa always said, when life deals you lemons, make lemon cocktails. In the case of Jesse's poker face, the man looked nervous all the time, even when he was collecting his winnings, so I had to fall back on another piece of advice my papa gave me.

Always raise when you have a full boat.

"I'll raise you fifty, Jesse," I said, tossing a handful of chips into the pot. True to his nature, Jesse neither blinked nor smiled. He simply tossed in a larger handful of chips than I did.

"I'll re-raise an even hundred," Jesse said, never taking his eyes off the pot. I found myself in that no-man's land that Texas Hold 'em players hate but know all too well. That special wilderness where you have just laid down too much cash to back off.

"I call," I said, feeling a dry scratchiness in the back of my throat. It was almost enough to cause me to reach for Jesse's pitcher of water, but that simply wasn't done. Still unsmiling and perspiring, Jesse laid down his hand.

"Two pair," Jesse said. "A pair of red jacks and a pair of black jacks."

I threw down my hand in disgust and got up from the table. Losing a hand is always bad enough, but nothing makes it worse than gambling wit. My stack was light about three hundred dollars, and most of that was in Sweet Jesse's pocket. I decided that I could use a break, and turned my attention to Sweet Jesse's sandwich tray while the other players took their turn as Jesse's punching bag.

When Sweet Jesse floats a game, the great consolation is that although your wallet is sure to be lighter, the spread he lays out for his games guarantees to satisfy.

Today the sweaty little toad stocked the bar with a nice selection of fancy Hefeweizens and Pilsners, and served them up with a hearty German Potato Salad and thick, warm Monte Cristo sandwiches. I used the edge of the table to pry open one of the ice cold bottles of beer, earning me a glare from a couple of the stiffs at the table. I shrugged and loaded my plate with enough potato salad to reach critical mass, tossing on a sandwich for good measure.

I watched the other players, Nick the Axe, Psycho Billy, and Barnstorming Pete Wilson push their chips around the table. They were just trading clay with each other as Sweet Jesse ate through them, piece by piece. While I ate, Jesse walked away with every pot but two, sweating and drinking his ice water through it all. Or so I thought.

On the next hand, the dealer flopped a seven, ten, and a jack. Billy checked his cards while the other seat holders mucked their hands. All but Sweet Jesse. Jesse raised twenty-five bucks, and without blinking Billy raised fifty.

The check-raise is an excellent poker strategy, and one of the few times when I feel it is acceptable for a player to check. As soon as Billy threw in his fifty, Sweet Jesse knew that Billy either had the nuts or wanted Jesse to believe that he did. Either way, Jesse threw in his money and they were playing poker.

The turn was a four, which probably did no one any good. Billy threw in a hundred more, daring Jesse to call. Jesse continued to sweat, took a drink of his ice water, and called. The dealer threw down a deuce.

Billy bounced, going all in, practically throwing in about two hundred more in chips. Even though this was a paltry sum compared to Sweet Jesse's stack, the big guy sat, sipping his water, and shuffling his chips. After a moment, he called Billy again, and Billy threw down an eight and a nine, giving him a straight. Sweet Jesse threw out a few curse words with his cards, drained his ice water, and motioned for one of his cronies to re-fill him.

Jesse didn't spend much time playing on tilt after losing. The next three hands all went to the fat man in succession, and he even threw down his hole cards when he took Billy's money, an arrogant move that I always detest in players.

Jesse was back to his winning form after his setback, sweating his way through the cheaply upholstered chair and winning a blue streak. I helped myself to a little more potato salad and another of the Monte Cristo sandwiches while I watched Sweet Jesse pluck himself some pigeons. I don't usually drink much during poker games, but the salt of the salad had given me a powerful thirst, so I cracked open another beer. The light Pilsner felt like heaven on my scratchy throat, and I could understand why Jesse kept draining that water pitcher next to him as he played. Except now I noticed that he didn't. Not since that last losing hand.

"Are you gonna stand there all day and raid my sandwich tray or are you going to play?" Sweet Jesse demanded. I filled my plate up with two more of the delicious, warm Monte Cristos and sat back down at the table.

I most certainly was going to play.

Between Sweet Jesse and me, Nick and Pete fell out of the game quickly, with most of their money split pretty evenly between us. Psycho Billy held out the longest, his stack being the biggest since he had taken a bite out of Jesse with his straight. Billy was a confident player, and confidence was always dangerous for someone.

"Full house," smiled Billy as he laid down his cards after going all in. "Sixes over tens." I smiled back at the dope and laid down my hand. His full house was enough to go all in in most circumstances, but not in all.

"Aces over sixes," I said, having a bigger boat than his. I swept the chips towards me as Billy rose from the table, put on his hat and coat, and tipped his chapeau to Sweet Jesse and me on his way out. I told Jesse that Billy took his losses well for a guy with the moniker of "Psycho."

"He's a big Hitchcock fan," snapped the fat man as he mopped Lake Erie off his forehead. "Are you in or not?"

"Sure," I said, reaching over to the sandwich tray to swipe the last Monte Cristo. I raised an eyebrow to my host before taking a bite.

"Go ahead," he grumbled, looking at his watch and dabbing his forehead again. "Christ, it's a quarter to five already!"

"Time flies," I tried to say, which came out of my full mouth as mumbles. Sweet Jesse nodded absently and flipped his chips. Our pots were evenly matched at about ten grand each.

"In that case, tough guy, I say we raise the blinds up to $500 and a grand," growled Jesse, confidence and sweat pouring from him. It didn't escape my notice that he said this when I was the big blind.

"Sounds good," I replied. "But if I win, you also throw in your Monte Cristo recipe."

"Sure, sure," he mumbled, eyeing my chips as if they were… well, a tray of sandwiches. "Just button your lip and play."

Jesse and I went heads up for about an hour, with him shoving some of his chips my way and me shoving some of mine to him. It was an exercise in futility, and never once did the big, sweaty mug take a drink. Things continued that way until about six thirty in the morning. Dawn had broken and my mouth had a nasty, stale taste in it. Jesse was his usual moist self, but a smile had broken out on the fat man's face.

"Tell you what," said the big guy, mopping his forehead. "It's past my bed time, so what do you say to getting down to business and making the blinds two and four grand?"

It was outrageous, and once again it would have made me the big blind, but seeing how we were out of sandwiches and beer, I decided that glory never went to the faint of heart.

"Fine," I told Jesse. "Let's play some poker."

The dealer threw two cards each at us and I saw that I had a pair of jacks. Or, as I call them, a sucker's hand. Not good enough to win most of the time, but good enough to make you believe that you had something. Across the table, Jesse dabbed his forehead and peeked at his hand.

"I'll see and raise three grand," he said nonchalantly, tossing in most of his chips. I watched his mug, figuring that he must have had better than my jacks. He sat motionless as the sweat ran down his chins, and his water glass remained untouched.

"I'll call," I sighed, hoping for another jack on the flop. What greeted me was not very welcome to either of us. A deuce, five, ten. Whatever we had in our hands was what we were playing.

I bet a grand, which in these circumstances is almost as bad as checking. Jesse pushed in a grand as well, and we both waited to see what bad news came up.

The dealer threw a jack onto the table, leaving me with trips, which would beat anything Sweet Jesse was holding. Suspecting he might hold queens or better, I threw in another grand, leaving us still evenly matched with five grand. He threw in another grand to call, and I noticed that the water still lay untouched.

The river card came and with it brought potential disaster. The dealer turned up an ace. If I was right about Sweet Jesse's pocket aces, I was dead. If he only had a pair of kings as hole cards, however, I would clean him out. I looked down at my anemic stack of chips and checked, broadcasting weakness. Jesse peeked under his hole cards, as if they had somehow changed in the minutes since he last looked. He then turned his gaze up to stare at me, and sat like a fat, sweaty statue.

"I say we call an end to this evening," he said after a moment, pushing the remainder of his chips into the pile. "All in."

I did my best not to blink, grit my jaw, or even breathe as Sweet Jesse wiped his forehead and waited for me to make my play.

Like me, Jesse knew the score. He also knew that I figured if he was holding the pocket aces, he would win. And whether he was or not, only he knew.

There was a hot, sweaty eternity between us as I stalled, counting chips, looking at my hole cards, and dividing three-hundred and nine by seventeen in my head I was hoping for any sign that Sweet Jesse was ready to crack.

Finally he did.

I called as Sweet Jesse took the most refreshing drink of ice water I had ever seen in my life.

# SWEET JESSE'S MONTE CRISTO SANDWICH

4 large eggs

1/4<sup>th</sup> cup of whole milk

2 teaspoons sugar

2 tablespoons hot sauce

½ teaspoon cinnamon

2 tablespoons Dijon mustard

12 slices thick, heavy sandwich bread

6 slices Swiss cheese

12 or so slices of thin deli ham

12 slices of thin turkey

3 tablespoons oil for pan

6 tablespoons strawberry preserve, served on the side of each sandwich

- In a shallow bowl, mix the eggs, milk, sugar, hot sauce, and cinnamon. On your workspace, build a pile of sandwiches out of your Dijon mustard, bread, cheese, ham, and turkey. Try not to be bashful with the cold cuts.

- Heat oil over medium heat, and dredge your sandwiches through the egg mixture, coating both sides of the sandwich. Fry on each side until both are a light brown.

- Serve them up with the strawberry preserves on the side, and make sure that you make enough for you, your guests, and any flatfoot that might happen to raid your game.

# THE CASE OF VINTAGE LARCENY

*Thefts occur, losses are suffered, and meats are tendered.*

I t was a hot, sticky, miserable day when Marcel Robest drifted into my office, making a bad day worse. I knew of Robest from what I gleaned from the society pages before I wrapped my garbage in them. Men such as Robest were referred to as "men of leisure" in polite society, or what my Ma would have referred to as lazy good-for-nothings. They were the guys with so much loot that they didn't even have to pretend to work. Their species wasn't usually spotted before four in the afternoon, and they tended to stalk their prey until the wee hours of the morning. Still, he stunk with wealth, so I sat up and willed my suit to look as if I hadn't taken it off the hanger three days before.

"What can I do for you?" I asked the pudgy, middle-aged swell with the dapper salt-and-pepper hair. He sat down in the chair I reserve for the paying guests and raised his nose disapprovingly, his refined olfactory senses used to better than the five-and-dime's best cologne. I shifted forward in my seat and paid close attention to what the man with the fat wallet had to say.

"I want you to find a bottle of wine for me," he said curtly, pulling a handkerchief from his breast pocket and waving it beneath his nose.

"I think you made a wrong turn at Fifth and Elm. This isn't Joe's Bar and Grill."

"The wine I seek," said Robest, ignoring my attempt at wit, "is a single bottle of Henri O'liveri Madeira. It is of a 1791 vintage and was bottled in 1841." His eyes took on a look of someone who had loved and lost, but in his case, the loss might have held some recycle value.

"And why exactly do you want this bottle?" I asked, suspecting that the answer might be a bit unseemly.

"It is MY bottle!" said the fat man, slamming a dainty fist onto my desk in way of punctuation. "It was stolen from my personal cellar and I want it returned to me!" He slipped his hand off of my desk and held it away from my sight. I paid him the courtesy of pretending not to notice him rubbing a bruised hand.

"I see," I said, opening up a notebook and pulling an attentive expression from my repertoire. "I take it your bottle of booze is pretty rare?"

"The grapes of this particular wine were harvested during the lifetime of Marie Antoinette," he said in a conspiratorial tone. "A case was given to Queen Victoria as a birthday present, and this particular bottle of 'booze,' as you call it, was given to Sir Winston as a thank you for services rendered to the crown." His eyes shone with the zeal of my least favorite uncle, a mug that spends every holiday trying to introduce me to religion. "To lose such a prize is an abomination."

"I follow you," I said. "And how did you manage to get your hooks on such a prize?"

"How I came to own it is of no matter," he said, snapping out of it. "What is important is that the bottle come back to me."

"So that you can drink an old bottle of wine?" I asked, imagining a very expensive salad dressing in a dusty glass coffin.

"So that I can possess an ancient treasure!" he hissed, his eyes narrowing. It didn't take much to picture Robest slithering into the garden selling apples. "That bottle of wine, it isn't to drink. It is to own."

I told the fleshy little glutton that he had himself an agent, and named the highest price I could think of. He agreed without a second thought, and it made me regret that I couldn't come up with a bigger number. Robest might have been off his hotdog, but his money was green.

I spent the day interviewing the help. It came to no one's surprise that most of his employees couldn't stand the smug bastard, and if I were Robest I would have thought twice before I chowed down on tonight's seafood bisque. Despite their apparent hatred of the man, they all seemed crystal clear on who paid the bills. The picture they painted of Robest was of a secretive, greedy man who wasn't in the habit of sharing anything with anyone. No one in his employ was familiar with any of the contents of his wine cellar, let alone the priceless bottle that lay inside. I had grilled them like halibuts, and came away with the feeling that each of them had as much a chance to find the bottle of Madeira as they would of better employment. But what they lacked in enological knowledge, they made up for in spades in the gossip department.

The evening the bottle went missing from Robest's cellar, he had hosted a small dinner party for an intimate group of sycophants, catered by a young, up-and-coming chef in the city. The dinner was designed to showcase Robest's wine cellar and pair some of his treasures with culinary creations created to rub his fortune in the faces of those who attended. From all accounts, he did just that, and the foie gras had left an ashen taste in the attendee's mouths.

Robest's valet gave me the name of the half-dozen or so envious souls in attendance that evening, as well as letting loose a lot of venom he kept in reserve from his boss. Apparently there was nothing that Robest did that didn't offend his staff. If I was the fat man, I might inspect my toothbrush before next using it.

I left Robest's household feeling a little dirty but armed with a short list of people who could have made off with the Madeira that evening. I considered stopping by my apartment to wash some of the disdain off me before I moved on, but I figured the quicker I solved this case, the quicker I could dab a little cash behind each ear.

The thing I just love about society swells is that they all believe in their heart of hearts that they are better than you. Perhaps it's money, perhaps it's breeding, perhaps it's the soft, doughy hands that have never even so much as touched an honest day's work. Whatever the reason, they seem down-right shocked whenever you have occasion to lay your hands on them. I might be generalizing, but so far a well-placed slap or a bent finger has loosened the tongue of many of the city's most upstanding citizens, and it was a belief which I hoped would continue to serve me.

I made a quick list of suspects from Robest's soirée, and had a quicker job of crossing each name off said list. To a person, each of the hoi-polloi had a witness who could vouch for them, could prove that they never made it into the cellar, or couldn't tell Madeira from mud water. They were simply there to taste the food that Robest had set out for them and to be seen. At the end of a long, brutal day, I had nothing but an exhausted list and bruised knuckles to show for it. I rolled the dice and came up snake–eyes.

I returned to the office to wrap up some loose ends and to call Robest and tell him that he could keep all his great-smelling cash, when suddenly I got a tip in the form of an empty, growling stomach.

I had yet to speak to the celebrity chef.


Chef Martin LaRue was known in the trades as "the Big Man." While I was a little on the chunky side, LaRue was down-right solid, built like a line-backer, and ready to throw fear into the suspension of even the heartiest taxi. He ran a catering business out of a swank little café he owned on the West Side. Café LaRue was the current flavor of the month, and at nine o'clock the line was around the block with people who had hopes of getting a table so that they could tell all their friends that they had gotten a table. The guy who guarded the front door looked like the guy who might guard the front door of Fort Knox, so I decided to try a more direct approach.

I made my way around the building and through the trash-strewn alleys behind the Café LaRue, looking for the service door. The door was unlocked, and someone who looked to be the sous chef was enjoying a cigarette. From behind him blared the maddening sounds of a busy kitchen, where every second word was a curse word and the ones in between were French. It would be easier to catch the chef here, in his own element.

I just had to keep my eyes open for the butcher's knife.

I made my way inside, where the racket and the chaos were at its thickest. Chef LaRue was at the center of his kingdom, shaking pans and stirring pots on at the range, and barking orders over his shoulder. I put a hand on the big man, and as I did, every action in the break-neck kitchen ceased, and the kitchen fell silent.

"Hello, my dear detective," said Chef LaRue, as if we were old chaps from the culinary academy. "How may I be of service to you?"

"You could start by telling me how you knew I would be turning up here," I asked.

"Monsieur Robest has been running all about town, squealing like a stuck pig about how his precious Madeira had been stolen during dinner," he said in the same tone he might take as if discussing the price of snails. "I thought it only be a matter of time before some cheap gumshoe might come knocking on my door." He dropped the spoon into his sauce and turned to look at me.

"No offense," he offered. I looked down at my trench coat and well-worn shoes.

"None taken," I said. "Now if you would be so kind as to spill the Cassoulet regarding the expensive vino, we can wrap this up quickly."

"My dear detective," said LaRue, feigning hurt feelings. "Surely you cannot suspect Chef LaRue of such chicanery?"

"Cut the baloney, Big Man," I said, grabbing him by the collar of his chef's jacket and yanking him towards me. "I know that Robest invited you into his cellar and I know that you know your wines!"

"Of course I know my wines," smiled the chef. "I'm French!" He slapped me on the shoulder and his smile widened. "But please, if we are to continue this conversation, allow us to do so away from the kitchen." He turned towards the assistants in the kitchen, and they all turned away from the Frenchman and flew into a flurry of activity, looking everywhere but into the eyes of the chef. He opened the door leading to the front of the house and bid me enter. He led me to a quiet corner in the back of the dining area, and we sat.

I was impressed that the Big Man didn't intimidate easily. Even more so because he was French. He snapped his fingers and the chef's assistant brought two glasses of wine and set them at our table. He raised a glass in salute.

"This isn't the wine…?"

"The Madeira?" he asked, laughing. "Before dinner? I think not." He took a gulp of the wine and let it slide down his throat, and I decided to do the same. I'm more of a whiskey guy myself, but when in Rome…or in this case Paris….

"Besides," added the chef in between drinks. "I have no idea where the priceless Madeira has got to." As we drank, LaRue's assistant brought in a plate of vegetables roasted in olive oil and topped with what the Fat Man called 'shaved truffles.' All I know is that it melted in my mouth.

"I know that you are hunting for the famous bottle of '41 Medeira, and you believe that the bottle is in my possession. I assure you that supposition is completely false."

"Issat so?" I replied, doing my best not to shoot the roasted veggies across the table and onto my host.

"Indeed," replied the Big Man. He snapped his fingers and a servant took the veggies away before I could lick the plate clean. A clanking sound came from somewhere in the place my heart should have been. Much to my relief, the waiter replaced my veggies with steak and potatoes.

"If you like, I will indeed open both my house and the restaurant stores to you, so that you can see that I do not possess the bottle that poseur Robest cherishes so much."

"Really?" I asked, genuinely surprised. "And if I kept an eye on you to make sure that no priceless wines came up on the market….?"

"You would not find my hand in any such matter. In fact, it is my belief that the bottle of Medeira doesn't even exist!"

"How do you figure that?" I asked, cutting into the steak. I took a bite of the succulent, reddish-brown flesh and felt my eyes roll into the back of my head. With another bite, I would have to rethink my views on religion.

"Robest is a blow-hard and a cretin. I'm sure he simply fabricated the story of the wine in order to increase his sorry reputation."

"You don't seem too fond of him," I said, cutting another piece off of the steak and savoring it. It was so tender that I could have cut it with a manila envelope.

"Take a lesson from the French, detective," the Big Man said as he drained the last of the wine from his glass. "Life is to be lived, women are to be loved, food eaten and wine savored. Anyone who would spend a fortune on such a bottle and never drink it is either a fool or a miser. And I have patience for neither."

"And should I see that particular bottle up for auction in London two months from now....?" I said.

"Watch me as long as you like, detective. My life is an open book. Just remember what I said and live life to the fullest."

"I'll do that," I told the Big Man as I finished my meal. Tomorrow I would go see Robest and tell him that I found neither cork nor label of his fine Portuguese vino. I'd still bill the pasty little weasel for the time I had spent on his behalf, but as with most of my clients, I doubted the funds would come. But that was tomorrow, and as the Fat Man said, I enjoyed life while I could.

"I'll try to take your advice," I told the large chef. "And I have to say that this is the finest meal I've ever eaten!"

"Music to my ears!" said the chef. "The secret is in the marinade!"

# Purloined Red Wine Marinade

1 lb. skirt steak

2 ½ cups leftover red wine

1 onion, diced

4 cloves of garlic, smashed

Juice from one lemon

1 whole sprig of rosemary

¼ cup olive oil

1 teaspoon salt

1 teaspoon pepper

- Sweet-talk your butcher into taking his thumb off the scale and giving you one of the cuts of meat that he gives to his friends and loved ones. Take it home, give it a quick trim to remove the gristle and some of the fat, and park it. In a shallow bowl, toss in the remaining ingredients and beat with a whisk as if you were expecting a confession. Submerge the steak and leave it overnight in the fridge.

- The next day, preheat a cast iron skillet to high, let the steak rest until room temperature, and then sear it on both sides. Cook until the center reaches the temperature you like and let it rest once again for ten.

Pure hard-boiled bliss!

# THE CASE OF THE BITING SPICE

*Sometimes the spice you don't know about has the most kick*

It was a rare sunny day in the city and the warmth spread like a fever. I started the day with a breakfast at Leo's Diner which consisted of crepes and coffee so strong it could sit up and beg. I followed up breakfast with a trip to the newsstand to pick up the daily rag, and then a stop at the local green grocer for a bag of farm fresh tomatoes. The plan for the day was to add the tomatoes to some ground beef that I had in the ice box, mix in some beans I had cooked the night before, and spend the day cooking a pot of chili while I watched the grass grow. Sometimes the absence of paying customers can be a blessing, especially during baseball season.

Now I make a pretty good pot of chili, but it's always been a sore point that it was good, not great, chili. I chalk it up to being a life-long Easterner. Years earlier, when Horace Greeley told Americans to "go west," my ancestors told him where to go right back.

I was in the kitchen, listening to the game and looking through my spice rack for inspiration to jump out at me, when my phone rang.

"Acme Chili Company," I said. "We like it hot."

"Why aren't you in your office?" shouted the voice on the other end. Long ago I had gone into business for myself just so I wouldn't have to answer questions like that.

"You can't expect a lug to be toiling away in a dank little office on a beautiful day like today." I told the troll-like voice, which I recognized as being attached to an equally troll-like body. "Besides, I don't work on Saturdays."

"It's Friday," growled the troll. "A hot-shot detective like you ought to have a clue about the days of the week." A quick glance at the calendar told me that the gruff voice had a point, so I shut up and listened for once. The voice, as I well knew, belonged to Lazlo Lavage, a bondsman with an office on the East side of town. Lazlo made a living off posting bail for the desperate and charging them inordinate prices later. He made a killing off bleeding those who were struggling just to get by, and he kept a long list of heavy hitters ready to track down those who skipped out on him. There were a few who made it past his goons and kept going, though. Those were the cases where Lazlo employed mugs like me.

Lazlo told me the story of Maria Del Toro, a small-time seamstress in the neighborhood, who posted a bond with Lazlo. She had disappeared about a week ago, and his people had seen neither hide nor hair of her since. He left her picture in my office, where he was forced to slide the envelope under the door since I had called in on account of being too healthy. She was in the wind, and Lazlo wanted me to get her back quickly.

"What did she do?" I asked the troll, wanting to know if I was going after a jaywalker or a mass-murderer.

"None of your business is what she done!" growled Lazlo. "When I was at your office earlier I didn't exactly notice a line of schmoes waiting to hire you." Once again the man had a point.

"And what are you offering," I said, casting a quick glance at my bag of tomatoes.

"The usual," he said.

"And?" There was a long pause on the phone as Lazlo mulled this over.

"Fine!" he barked. "I'll pay your expenses and give you a $100 bonus!"

"And?" I asked. I could tell that I was in imminent danger of causing Lazlo's head to explode.

"And what!" he screamed. "What else do you want? The moon?!?"

As I said, I made a good pot of chili, but Lazlo on the other hand…. "I believe you know what, my friend."

"Fine!" he yelled. I was beginning to think that Lazlo did not possess an 'indoor voice.' "I'll give you my chili recipe as well! Just find Maria. And make it snappy!" Lazlo slammed the phone down, and I was left with very little to go on.


Making a quick stop by my office to pick up the envelope Lazlo slid under the door, I did my best to dope out Maria's whereabouts.

The envelope held only Maria's picture, and it verified that she was indeed a knock-out. The paperwork that Lazlo kept on everyone he did business with was conspicuously missing. Usually I would have called Lazlo back and asked him for more info, but he had already made it clear that I was there to find Maria and keep out of his business.

Since I knew absolutely nothing about one Maria Del Toro, the natural place for me to start was at the precinct house on the East Side. I was on the permanent list of "persona non grata" there, so I waited around the corner at O'Malley's, a cop bar, for a friendly face to stop in. It took a while, and I had to endure many a sarcastic comment about peeping into windows or tracking down lost pooches. I fended off the remarks by saying that my confidentiality agreement prevented me from telling them what their wives had to say about them.

Luckily for me, I didn't have to languish too long inside the bar before a friendly face in the form of Mike McCarthy, Special Investigator for the District Attorney, appeared. Mike saw that I was about to be shown the ugly side of a bartender's baseball bat and jumped in to save me.

"Back off guys," Mike told the off-duty coppers. "He isn't worth your time."

"You can say that again," grumbled one of the flat-footed mugs as they all made their way back to the bar. Mike told me that I owed him one, and I decided to press my luck by showing him the photo of Maria Del Toro.

"She's quite a dish," Mike told me, "but she hasn't been charged with anything."

"Are you sure?" I asked, falling into my usual state of confusion.

"Do you think I would forget a face like this?" he asked. "Particularly with the Dick Tracy Rogues Gallery I usually work with?"

Mike had a point, but I asked him to keep looking and get back to me if he found anything. I bought him a beer and decided to hot-foot it out of the bar before I was charged with something. I was back at square zero, seeing as my client wasn't exactly fluent in the truth. But there was still a part of the story that I could follow up on. And if I was lucky, I might even have my jacket let out a bit.

The place where Maria Del Toro worked as a seamstress was in the Nickel District, and in the Nickel, there were only two types of seamstresses. The first were the ones who worked in the shops owned by uptown tailors who sent their work down here to get it done cheaply for their rich clients. The second were the seamstresses who did work for mortuaries.

After knocking on lots of doors and wearing out a little shoe leather, I found that Maria Del Toro was a seamstress for one of those uptown swells. The building she worked at was a run-down sweatshop that employed somewhere in the neighborhood of twenty woman. The flea that owned the shop paid the women pennies an hour while charging the uptown hoi-palloi top dollar. It was good work if you could get it, and you could sleep at night once you got it. I could try charging in and questioning these women, but I knew places like this. Every one of the ladies knew that, if they spoke to a shamus like me, they would be out of work five minutes later. If I were to go in there heavy with a lot of questions, then the only thing I would accomplish would be getting the dames to dummy up and probably getting them all fired in the process.

I got a bratwurst and coffee from a shop up the road, as well as a newspaper. I planted myself on a park bench across the street from the sweatshop and waited. The ability to wait, along with the ability to stomach dreadful coffee and bratwurst, is a job requirement. I opened up the paper to the box scores, sipped on some coffee, and waited.

I warmed the park bench for almost three hours before a loud horn sounded somewhere in the building, signaling the end of the work day. The women filed out in groups of two or more, moving slowly, too tired to make the walk home let alone work up any enthusiasm about it. I waited for stragglers, and saw my opening when one of the ladies left the building by herself.

She was thin, dark-haired, middle-aged, and as skittish as a kitten when she left the building, looking over her shoulder. She was making sure that she wasn't being followed, and doing everything but wearing a "please follow me" sign as she did so. She was as innocent as a babe when it came to spotting a tail, and she mistook me for just another schmoe enjoying his brats in the park.

I followed her, watching as she stayed in the shadows and took to the back alleys. She walked almost three blocks out of her way and back-tracked to a small studio located in the rear of a local bakery. The dame looked this way and that before she made her way into the apartment. I felt a little bad that she wouldn't know if anyone was following her unless it was a marching band. The door cracked open and the seamstress slipped in, darkness enveloping her, as the door closed. I walked around the building, as well as the bakery, just to make sure that this wasn't more of the lady's shenanigans. Then I played the waiting game once more, partly because I was still on Lazlo Lavage's dime, but mostly because when I'm tailing someone I don't like surprises.

The sky filled with the kind of darkness that was all around this case, and after a while someone inside the small apartment flipped on a light. I snuck closer to the front door, and I could hear the sounds of two female voices. Neither voice sounded very serene. I listened for a while, getting pieces here and there in Spanish. After a few moments I decided that listening outside of women's doors wasn't doing loads for my self-image, so I took a chance and knocked.

There was plenty of shuffling and "shush"-ing going on in the small apartment, and after a minute or so everything went quiet. It was a shaky, frightened voice that came drifting through the door.

"Who is there?" the voice asked. I assumed that it was the woman I tailed from the seamstress shop.

"I'm looking for Maria Del Toro," I said, using my 'Voice of Authority.' It's the tone of voice I use when I want people who have no reason to talk to me to talk to me. In this case, the 'Voice of Authority' let me down. Inside there was more shushing and moving around and I heard a lamp break. It didn't take a genius to recognize the sounds of desperation and panic.

I moved away from the door and peered around the corner, to the only window the tiny apartment possessed. I saw a suitcase drop down, and the leg of a woman who was most certainly not the middle-aged seamstress I tailed to this studio. I moved to the window and, as the woman backed her way out of the apartment, I helped her down. My reward was a scream.

The young woman took a tumble backwards and fell into me. We both spilled onto the alleyway and the woman I tailed appeared before me, shotgun in hand. In other circumstances I would have jumped to my feet, but I was covered with a hysterical, crying younger version of the seamstress. I heard the older woman pull back the twin hammers of the shotgun as the younger woman peeled herself off me.

"Miss Del Toro?" I smiled. "I would like to provide you with full coverage for all your life insurance needs."

Then I felt the butt of a shotgun strike the side of my head, and what little light was there went out.


I came to in the alleyway with the sharp taste of gun metal still fresh in my mouth. From somewhere nearby I could hear two voices arguing frantically, and it occurred to me that I hadn't been out too long. Certainly not as long as the two seamstresses had hoped. I continued to lay in the dirt and grime of the alley, playing dead. From underneath my body I slowly snaked my hand into the holster under my left arm. I had been lucky all through this case, and my luck had continued to hold. I was clearly dealing with amateurs. The ladies were trying to get out of Dodge while the shady character they had koncked on the noggin lay sleeping it off. They didn't tie me up and they never even checked to see if the shady character had a gun. The shady character did.

The women might have been rank amateurs, but I hadn't exactly handled myself like a pro thus far. As my hand found its way around the grip of my pistol, I decided that I was through letting luck decide my fate. Luck had a nasty way of kicking you when and where you least expected it. It was time I trusted in a higher power.

"All right," I said, struggling to my feet as I aimed a shaky snubnose at the ladies. "I don't know exactly what's going on here, but my head is throbbing, I'm dirty, and I've spent the last two days peeking in people's windows. Now I just have one question. Which one of you is Maria Del Toro?"

The ladies stopped in their tracks, dropped the suitcase, and looked at each other, waiting to see who would crack first. I gave them a moment before I cleared my throat, and the young woman in the shadows stepped forward, revealing herself to be the young woman from the photo.

"I am Maria Del Toro," she said, her voice trembling.

"Pleased to meet you, Miss Del Toro," I said, reaching out and taking the shotgun from the older woman. "I believe that you and I have much to discuss."

The older woman with Maria turned out to be her Aunt, and Maria had been lying low for the last week or so until she could arrange passage to her mother's home in Arizona. When I asked about Lazlo Lavage, both Maria and her aunt broke into hysterics. Lazlo had never posted a bond for Maria, and she had never committed any crime. Lazlo's interest in Maria was much more unsavory than that.

Maria told me that she met Lazlo when he had visited the sweatshop she worked in, looking for a skip. He was smitten at first glance and somehow she had managed to keep her lunch down. Maria confessed that she had dated Lazlo for a few months, a feat which I considered either charitable or naive. She had seen Lazlo as a rich and powerful man, which I guess I could see if I squinted hard enough. She also told me that Lazlo was hooked on her from day one, which didn't require bifocals.

She went on to spin me a fairy tale about how Lazlo wined and dined her, showered her with gifts, and promised her the moon. Maria went on with her story while Auntie got me a glass of water and apologized for bashing me on the noggin with a 12-guage. It wasn't the first time. I grunted something in the way of acceptance and the older woman kept an eye on me as she started straightening the apartment. Straightening and packing.

Maria's story continued all hearts and flowers for a while, until reaching the act where Lazlo turned mean. Anyone who had known Lazlo longer than a New York minute knew that was Lazlo's natural state, and I can only assume that Maria was blinded, if not by love, then at least a love of the things that Lazlo would provide her.

Lazlo made demands and his temper flared, turning him from Prince Charming to Frankenstein's Monster. Maria tried to walk out on him a few times, but Lazlo wasn't having any of it. He made that clear to her one starry evening when he told her that if she left him, she would get the 'Marbles' Monroe treatment.

To this day, 'Marbles' mother still wears black when she so much as goes out for a quart of milk.

"Angela was the only family I had here. My mother lives in Sedona. I lived with Aunt Angela since I moved here a year ago, but Lazlo's men know where she works." She leaned forward and grabbed my forearm with a grip that had been built by years of needlework. "Please, my aunt and I need to disappear before Lazlo finds us. We need to get out of the city."

"Maria," said Aunt Angela in a sad, beaten tone. "Senior Lazlo's men have already found us."

Both of the women fell silent and looked at each other. I sighed and held up a hand to calm them before they got out of hand and tried to kill me again.

"I'm not one of Lazlo's men," I protested.

"So you weren't hired to find Maria to take her back?" asked the aunt hopefully.

"Uh…well, I kind of was," I started, sparking off much wailing and shouting, much of it in Spanish.

"Whoa, whoa," I said, putting away my pistol and holding out both hands. "I'm not a flunky, I'm a detective." The ladies stopped at this, but the looks on their faces told me that they didn't see a natural distinction between the two. Most days, I'm not sure that I do either.

I told Maria and Aunt Angela that I was hired by Lazlo because she had skipped out on bail. Maria confirmed what Mike from the DA's office told me. She'd never had so much as a jaywalking ticket, let alone bail posted for her. Lazlo wanted a shamus just smart enough to find his lady, but not smart enough to ask any questions. I decided to get off the stupid train here and now.

"My plan isn't to hand you over to Lazlo," I told the frantic women. I had to repeat it a couple of times in order to get them to slow down and relax, but eventually my words penetrated.

"It isn't?" asked a wide-eyed Maria. "Why?"

I could have told her that I don't like being lied to by a client, any client, and I could have told her that taking a case from Lazlo Lavage already left a bad taste in my mouth that even his chili couldn't erase. I also could have told her that I don't think I could sleep at night if I delivered her and her auntie to a slug such as Lavage. I told her none of that.

"It ain't my style, sister," I said, and that was pretty much that.

I watched Maria and Aunt Angela finish packing up their belongings and loading up the beat-up sedan parked in front of the bakery. As I helped them strap on the last of their second-hand luggage, Maria asked what it would cost me to let her go. I told her about the payment and the expenses, but the part that really hurt was the recipe. It looked as if I were going have to wing my next batch of chili.

Maria smiled and went back to the apartment one last time. As Aunt Angela secured the last of their belongings, Maria returned and started to tell me where in Arizona they were headed.

"Save it, sister," I warned her. "I don't want you to tell a soul where you're going until ten minutes after you're there, understand?"

Maria nodded, her big cow eyes filling with tears. She and her aunt gave me a hug so tight that I saw stars for a moment, and then I felt something being pressed into my hand. Aunt Angela smiled wide, spoke quickly, and said lots of stuff. Most of it was in Spanish, some of it in English, and none I understood. I nodded back to her as she got into the passenger side of the sedan. Maria once again thanked me for what I considered as my only human act of the day, and kissed me softly on the cheek. From that kiss alone I could see what Lazlo saw in her, and it brought me no small amount of satisfaction to make sure that she escaped his greasy mitts.

They drove off into the sunset, aunt and niece, and as they did so I smiled in a way that I hadn't for a long time, and probably wouldn't again for a while. When the ladies had disappeared into the horizon, I looked down into my hand and examined the note Maria had slipped me. It was a hastily written recipe, along with a message scribbled at the top.

"Who do you think gave Lazlo the recipe in the first place?"

Perhaps good deeds are rewarded after all.

# Maria's Chili con Carne

3 dried ancho chilies

1 to 3 tablespoons vegetable oil

4 ounces pork shoulder, finely chopped

2 pounds boneless chuck steak, cut into 1/2-inch cubes

1 large white onion, chopped (2 cups)

3 cloves garlic, minced

1 teaspoon ground cumin

1 teaspoon dried oregano

1 bay leaf

Kosher salt

28 ounces whole peeled tomatoes, briefly pulsed in a blender

2 bottles of cheap beer

1 tablespoon white vinegar

- Take the dried chilies and dump them into a skillet, cooking over medium heat for about two minutes or until they start to puff up. Remove the cores and seeds, putting the seeds aside. Put the chilies in a bowl and cover them with boiling water. Put them aside.

- Heat one tablespoon of oil in a Dutch oven over medium heat. Add the pork and brown, then move and park it someplace convenient. Add the beef and brown it as well, working in batches. When you have completed that assignment, park it also.

- Put your chilies into a blender or food processor with about a half-cup of the hot water you soaked them in. Puree the chilies and set aside. Add the onion and garlic to the Dutch oven and cook for eight minutes or so. Stir in the cumin, oregano, bay leaf, and one tablespoon of salt. Toss in some of the reserved seeds to add a little heat to the enterprise. Cook for one more minute before you throw in the puree. Turn the heat to high and cook for two more minutes or so, stirring often.

- Return the meat to the pot and add two more teaspoons of salt, the tomatoes, and the beer. Bring the stew to a boil, then reduce the heat to medium for about one and a half hours, stirring occasionally.

- Reduce the pot to low heat, fish out the bay leaf, and stir in the vinegar until the meat is tender and your spirits are a little brighter. Dish you and your cronies up heaping bowls, and top them with some grated cheese, broken tortilla chips, or dashed dreams. Whatever floats your boat.

# The Case of the Awkward High Note
*Do Re Me Coq Au Vin*

W hen I was a kid, the gargoyles at the Metropolitan Opera gave me nightmares. Large, gaping stone mouths, bat wings, and leering faces that seemed to beg small children to stop by for a quick bite. My mom used to scrape up enough money to drag her kids there for a Saturday matinee of high class and culture, when all we really wanted was to see the Scarlet Gumshoe bust up a ring of racketeers in the weekly serials. Ma desperately wanted her kids to get an education, to appreciate the finer things and, for the most part, it worked. I learned at a young age how to tell Verdi from Mozart. That was the same year Billy Driscal saw my mom haulin' us out of the Met one afternoon and he told all the kids in my class that I loved the opera.

That was also the year I learned to fight.

Steven Gomez

I never developed the appreciation of opera and culture that Ma hoped I would, but at least I learned not to let the gargoyles bother me. Except now, to my surprise, the Met had hired one of them to guard its door.

"I told you to shove off," said the ape someone crammed into a red doorman's jacket. I could only assume that the Met had paid some unfortunate tailor to extend the length of the arms on the jacket to simian proportions. He had taken about three steps closer to me than society deemed acceptable, and I got a strong whiff of the horseradish that accented today's roast beef special at the local deli.

"And I told you that Old Lady Bancroft is expecting me," I said to the primate. Inching closer to me, he started to roll up his sleeve. With sleeves like his, that would take quite a while.

I was taking a mental inventory of all the tender places on the goon's anatomy I could place a cheap shot before he tried to kill me. Luckily for me, before any shots were placed, cheap or otherwise, a voice rang out from somewhere behind Kong.

"Andrew!" came the cry, stopping the goon in mid-homicide. "This gentleman is my guest!"

Andrew immediately dropped his arms and stood straight, as if a drill sergeant had called him to attention. And I guess in a way, one had.

"Mrs. Bancroft!" Andrew stuttered. "I thought…"

"I don't imagine that you thought at all!" Mrs. Bancroft said in a frosty tone. "Otherwise you would not make me strain my voice before the season begins!" The voice in question, Mrs. Bancroft's, was

92

indeed a forceful and powerful weapon. And the package it was attached to wasn't a wilting flower either.

Mrs. Bancroft looked to be in her late fifties, stood about six-foot one, and had enough bulk on her to play middle linebacker when the Metropolitan was in off-season.

"Please follow me," Bancroft told me from behind the ape. Andrew shuffled off to the side, just enough to let me pass, his mouth gaping.

"You got a little of that horseradish on your lapel," I told him, pointing to his jacket. When he looked down, I zipped my finger upwards and gave him a chuck on the nose.

"Lead the way, Mrs. B," I told the woman, and she showed me down a long corridor towards the dressing rooms.

"You'll have to forgive Andrew," she told me over her shoulder. "He is the sentry of the grandest Opera House on Earth and is sometimes a little overzealous."

"Didn't he know you were expecting someone?" I asked.

"I told him I was expecting a guest," she said, opening the door to her dressing room. "I'm sure that he was expecting someone a bit…different."

She looked at my wrinkled suit as if it might crawl off my body and bite her.

"I'm sure he was," I said. "Now why don't you tell me what it is a mug like me can do for a dame like you?"

Bancroft sighed and collapsed onto a sofa-like structure. The sofa groaned a little, but held up its end of the bargain.

"I've asked you here on a matter of considerable…discretion." She looked put out, as if I had asked her if Rigoletto was a German opera, so I imagined that the matter was serious indeed.

"Lady, when you pay me, you also pay for my silence." It sounded remotely chivalrous, but if you go around spilling your client's secrets, soon you have no clients left. Mrs. Bancroft seemed relieved by my answer. The old bird sat up straight on her sofa, head held high, and addressed me in the manner of an elegant lady addressing the help.

"As you may know, I have spent many years at the forefront of European culture and have been an eminent champion of the Opera in the U.S."

"Do tell," I said, examining a little bit of the shipyards I had caught under my fingernails earlier that day. "Go on."

Clearing her throat, Mrs. Bancroft regarded me with the disdain of someone who wasn't worthy of washing her pet poodle, but she managed to soldier on.

"Anyway," she continued, "I am in the middle of financing this season's opening production of the Metropolitan Opera. This is a precarious junction for the Opera, and I have spent much of my personal fortune and reputation making sure that this season's Pagliacci is performed flawlessly." She paused, looking down over the frames of her pearl glasses, searching for understanding in my eyes. There was none.

"Pagliacci is a timeless story …" she sighed, as if she were explaining Calculus to sixth-graders.

"Yeah, yeah," I mumbled. "Everyone loves a clown."

That stopped her in her tracks, and her jaw dropped floor-wards. As I said, Ma used to drag me to the opera.

"Well, at any rate," Mrs. Bancroft muttered, regaining her composure. "I have invested heavily in this production, both in monetary and social equity, and I stand to lose substantially should anything disrupt this premiere."

I had to hand it to her. She certainly could talk up a storm.

"And is there any reason that this production could suffer…disruption?" I asked, and immediately regretted it. As soon as the words left my mouth, she broke down, sniffles, tears, and a strange 'neighing' sound erupting from her all at the same time. Her hand fluttered behind her, and it looked to me as though the old broad might swoon. I stood up quickly, figuring I might have to catch her before she hit the deck. As I maneuvered in behind her to try and catch the old bird, I had visions of hazard pay in my future. Luckily the old dame righted herself before I abused my sacroiliac.

She sat on the edge of her sofa and took a few deep breaths before she was able to speak. It was real emotion in her eyes when she turned back to me, instead of the fake society stuff that passed for it. I gave her a moment to wipe her tears and catch her breath before she spoke. When she did speak, it was as if a little girl had taken the place of the woman.

"Have you ever been guilty of a youthful indiscretion?" she asked me. I answered yes to the 'indiscretion' part, but no to the 'youthful.' She smiled an actual smile and continued.

"When I was a bit younger, and a bit more naive, I met a man. I was married to my late husband Randolph at the time, but this man was young, vigorous, and exciting." I imagined that they are all young, vigorous, and exciting when you are married to a mug like the late Randolph Bancroft.

"We made vows to each other. Promises were made, oaths were taken...."

"Letters were exchanged?" I added with a sigh.

"Letters were exchanged," she sighed back in resignation. In my trade, I've noticed that letters were always exchanged.

"The man for whom I had fallen vanished into the ether! He had asked for a thousand dollars to arrange for us to run away and have a fresh start. Another life, if you will. And on the day he was to come and collect me..." She broke down, and the words dried in her throat.

"He never showed."

"No," she sobbed. "He never came." She reached over and pulled a handkerchief from off of one of those chiffarobes, or highboys, or whatever the hell the society dames call those fancy little dressers. After a moment, she regained her composure.

"After Maurice left me..."

"Maurice?" I asked.

"Maurice." She answered. "After Maurice left, I resigned myself to making my marriage work. I finished my education and Randolph and I left for the continent. It was there I immersed myself in the life that is the opera. Randolph and I made the best of our lives, and fell once again into love. It was only after Randolph passed that I left the continent to return to the city."

With full control of the Randolph fortune, I thought. But the meter was running, and it was her dime.

"When I returned to my life in America," she continued, "I dedicated myself to the cause of bringing enlightenment to the deprived masses."

"By means of opera?" I asked.

"By means of opera."

"All was well as society welcomed me back with open arms. I found a place with the Met, and established myself as a driving force in the creative community." Her eyes had that far-way look, and for a moment, I feared she might break out in song. "Everything was falling into place in my life."

"Until...?" I interjected.

"Until the letters arrived," she sighed, and the faraway look in her eyes vanished, replaced by a here-and-now look of resignation. "Just one or two letters, but there were more letters out there, and they were by far more..." The words escaped her.

"And I am assuming that they came from Maurice?" I asked.

"Never!" she protested. "What Maurice and I shared was a special bond. A melding of the spirits! What we had he would never betray for filthy lucre! I can only assume that some tragedy has befallen Maurice. Our passion may have been star-crossed, but our love was eternal! He must have perished, and our letters fallen into unscrupulous hands."

"So," I said standing and making my way to the door. "You want me to find your blackmailer and ...?"

"And retrieve my letters!" she commanded. "I want to make sure that my good name remains untarnished and that the Metropolitan's season opens without scandal of any kind!"

"And if it turns out that old Maurice is the guy pulling the strings?" I ventured.

"Impossible!" she said, dismissing me as the help I guess I now was. "I want you to find this cretin and return to me the memories of my youth." She stood and turned her back to me, letting me show myself out. As I made my way back to the gorilla at the door, Mrs. Bancroft called to me from over her shoulder.

"Detective, if you have to give this ne'er-do-well a thrashing in the process, I shan't mind!"

It took me about fifteen minutes to find Maurice. His full name was Maurice De Leon, and he had kept anything but a low profile. Working through my list of contacts, I simply had to describe the slimy little weasel to Benny at Chez Petite Francois, cross his palm with a sawbuck, and Benny sang me a tune that was both enlightening and nauseating.

Maurice was a gold-digging hustler, but managed to keep his trade secret by virtue of his appearance. Although he was a short, sweaty, doughy, pug-like man, Maurice dressed in tailor-made suits that cost more than my annual rent, and adorned himself in jeweled tie-clips, pinkie rings, and watch fobs that defied imagination. If clothes made the man, then old Maurice was a prince.

Maurice, according to Benny, had never worked a day in his life but was accustomed to the finer things. He was often seen on the arm of rich, if not desperate, older women in society, and would feed off of them like a leech until the well ran dry or until marriage was unavoidable. Then he would run off in the night as fast as his fat little legs would carry him, often to greener and more lucrative, pastures.

I caught up to the snake as he was leaving the Leaping Lord, an old-fashioned, honest-to-goodness private club in the city. The Lord was an old-world joint that cost an arm and a leg to join, but apparently was a little lax on character requirements.

I tailed Maurice past the park, to a brownstone off Weber Street. The building was an impressive piece of architecture. It stood proudly near the great park, side-by-side with some of the finest homes in the city. Maurice had done well for himself after making Mrs. Bancroft's acquaintance on the continent. He had wealth, stature, and a place in the very society that Mrs. Bancroft was working her way towards.

It occurred to me that high society played a little lax with its character requirements as well.

Maurice entered the house, turned on a few lights, and made his way to the kitchen. As the rattle of the pots and pans grew, the smell of chicken and garlic wafted through the air. I pressed my face to the window, watching Maurice lay a bowl for himself and ladling it heavy with stewed chicken, onions, mushrooms, and wine. He sat the dish down on a small table in the kitchen, uncorked a bottle of Burgundy, and poured himself a healthy snootful. From there I watched him as he walked into the parlor and over to one of the many enormous bookshelves lining the walls of the room.. Each shelf overflowed with phonograph records. He studied the shelves as if he were going to be tested on them and, after some time, a smile pushed through his many chins as he pulled a record from the shelf.

Carrying the record as if it was his first born, he walked to the nearby oak chest and opened the lid, revealing a very elegant and very expensive phonograph. He carefully placed the record on the player, lowered the needle, and was rewarded with the powerful blast of an Italian tenor filling the house. He closed his eyes and smiled as he soaked in the music. It filled every part of him, almost lifting the pudgy little toad off the floor. He hovered for a few more moments in rapture before remembering his dinner.

Walking back through the small hallway that connected the parlor to the kitchen, Maurice paused at a framed playbill from a European opera hall. He quickly looked from his left to his right as I dove into the bushes, catching a mouthful of Hydrangea for my troubles. From the peeping tom position, I watched Maurice pull on the corner of the framed picture, revealing a wall safe on the other side. This complicated matters.

His considerable bulk blocked my view of his sausage-like fingers working the dial. When the door opened, he tossed in his wallet, his watch, and a few stray papers. From what little I could see in the safe, it looked as if most of its contents were paperwork. And most of the paperwork looked like stationery.

I began to doubt that Mrs. B was his only pigeon.

I watched Maurice return to his bowl of stew in the kitchen, and the muscles in my jaw tightened. The presence of the safe was an issue.

I couldn't just waltz in and slap the little weasel around for the letters. I could wait for Maurice to leave, but since Mrs. B was on his hook he might just decide to move the letters.

The time to strike was now, but I was coming up snake-eyes. I was tired, out of ideas, and my stomach was protesting the copious amounts of coffee I drank all day. To make matters worse, the scent of Maurice's chicken stew was intoxicating and my already rebelling gut gave a rumble in protest. I was about to call it an evening and find some grub when inspiration struck. It was after five o'clock and, down the street a newsboy was getting ready to start hawking the evening edition.

I rang Maurice's bell, using the time it took the portly man to waddle from his kitchen to the front door to straighten my tie and smooth my hair. I had dusted the dirt I collected from Maurice's shrubbery off my suit and managed to look presentable, but I knew that if you held my suit up next to Maurice's, mine was destined for the rubbish bin.

Maurice threw open the door and sized me up immediately. Since I obviously held little wealth, influence, or power, he kept his reserve of pleasantness closed, lest he run low on it at some critical moment.

"Waddaya want?" he said, small pieces of chicken raining down from his mouth onto my suit. Maurice clearly wasn't a man who enjoyed being disturbed in mid-feedbag.

"Mr. De Leon, I represent the owner of a small liquidation company, and I was referred to you by a fellow representative of the

Collins-Walker Listening Library." I had looked in the phonebook, and this was the most upscale library listed. "I have in my possession a small but very discerning listing of recordings from the continent, and it has been mentioned that someone of your refined tastes might appreciate such an offering."

"Recordings?" Maurice asked, finishing his mouthful and spotting the possibility of personal benefit. He cracked open the charm reserve and I was treated to a smile and a welcome.

"Where are my manners?" asked Maurice, stepping backwards and showing me inside. "I was just at dinner, but please, do come in."

Maurice led me to the kitchen where he pulled a chair out, poured a small glass of Burgundy, and asked if I would care to join him for a bowl of Coq au Vin. The smell in the small kitchen was heaven, and clearly Maurice knew his stuff. The man may very well have been a creep, a blackmailer, and a gold-digger, but he knew his way around a stove.

"Now please, tell me more about this collection of yours."

I gave him a fake name, using a couple of the names of streets I grew up on. I told him that my firm had acquired a number of rare pieces, including lost recordings of Luigi Mancinelli, Ezio Pinza, and Enrico Caruso. It was a lavish, lush, inviting picture I painted as I feasted on a Coq au Vin that was equally tasty. But there was one distinct difference between the collection I described and the tasty stew.

The collection didn't exist.

As I went on about the fabricated collection, Maurice's eyes seemed to narrow and his head nodded slightly, as if he were a snake about to strike. He refilled my wine glass as I greedily finished off my stew.

"This collection sounds remarkable," Maurice said, not wanting to show too many cards. I would have told him that it sounded too good to be true, but my mouth was full. "And the firm you represent is willing to part with this collection for ...?"

He wanted me to give a number so that he could counter it with half, or less. I wanted to give him a high number, so that he would feel that my collection actually existed. Before I had a chance to say anything, we were interrupted.

There was a knock on Maurice's door. To be more precise, there was a torrential rain of bangs and blows to the front door, mixed in with kicks and doorbell rings thrown in for good measure. Even if I had answered Maurice's question, my response would have been lost in the racket that came from his landing.

"What the blazes!" Maurice said as he sprang from his chair faster than I would have thought possible for a man of his bulk. He raced from his kitchen through the hallway and parlor, and around the corner to the front door. He threw the door open, preparing to rebuke the intruder for the loud and unwelcomed interruption, and found that the source of the racket was about three feet lower than he expected.

"Hey Mister!" yelled a young, freckle-faced Franklin Meyers, the newspaper boy from the end of the block. "Billy was supposed to pick up his load of papers from the docks and get them to me an hour ago! You gotta get him out here and put his butt in gear!"

Maurice stood transfixed, trying to decipher Franklin's words as if they were in a foreign tongue. Slowly his senses returned and he addressed the loud little newsy.

"Young man, there seems to be some sort of misunderstanding. I have no idea who or what you are looking for, but I assure you that you have the wrong house."

"Oh no you don't mister!" yelled Franklin as he jammed his foot into the door. "I've been down the block all morning pulling my own shift, and I ain't gonna pull another because Billy's too lazy to do his job. You tell him to get his sorry behind out here!"

Maurice attempted to reason with Franklin, and then tried to forcibly remove him. All the while the kid was screaming bloody murder. I had to hand it to the kid, he was earning the five-spot I gave him before I entered Maurice's home. So far, he had got Maurice out of the kitchen and arranged for me to spend some quality time with the wall safe. The rest was up to me.

The safe was a bare-bones type, with a large, numerical dial on the front, but it was enough to do the job. While I'm no expert, I've been able to crack the odd safe in favorable circumstances. The problem was, with Franklin yelling his lungs out at the front door, circumstances were less than favorable.

I gave the dial a few test spins, just enough to shake up the tumblers, and determined that it was a three-number combination. Quickly, I thought what numbers a music-nut like Maurice would use. Measures, octaves, and scales all floated through my head as I tried to latch onto something, but I was nowhere. I cursed myself. A golden opportunity was slipping through my fingers.

Then it hit me!

It wasn't a musical clue I was looking for at all. The combination came from Maurice's day job.

38-24-38.

I spun the dial and the safe opened like the Gates of Heaven for a just man. I quickly found the letters and was set to go when my eye caught sight of another prize. I pocketed the note that caught my eye, showed myself out through the parlor window, and was down the street fast enough to see Franklin blowing raspberries at Maurice as the fat man finally managed to dislodge the paperboy from his doorstep.

I met up with Franklin at his corner and gave him the second five-spot, as per our agreement. I also tossed him a fifty-cent piece as a bonus. As I made my way back to my own humble abode on the other side of the tracks, I imagined that I would sell Mrs. B some soft-soap about Maurice being lost at sea, or captured by cannibals, or some other tripe. The man was as easy to find as bad news, but she chose not to. She wanted more than just her reputation. She wanted to hold onto the memories.

I would meet her tomorrow at the Met after I tossed Andrew a banana or two. I would give her the letters and I would make a nice little profit on a less-than-honest day's work. But in the meantime, I had some chicken stew to whip up.

# MAURICE'S COQ AU VIN

1/2 lb. bacon slices, cut into ½" pieces

1 large yellow onion, sliced

3 lbs. chicken thighs and legs, excess fat trimmed, skin ON

6 garlic cloves, peeled

Salt and pepper to taste

2 cups chicken stock

2 cups Burgundy Red wine

2 bay leaves

Several fresh thyme sprigs

Several fresh parsley sprigs

2 cups button mushrooms, trimmed and roughly chopped

2 Tbsp. butter

Chopped Fresh parsley for garnish

- In a large Dutch oven, brown the bacon on medium heat, just long enough to fill the kitchen with the smell of heaven, or about ten minutes. Remove the cooked bacon but keep it handy.

- In the pot, working in small batches, add the chicken and onions, skin side down. Brown the bird well on all sides, adding salt and pepper as you go.

- Spoon off the excess fat and add the chicken stock, wine and herbs. Toss the bacon back in and bring the whole mess to a boil. Reduce the heat and simmer for twenty minutes. Cover the Dutch oven and cook until the bird is tender and cooked through. Remove the chicken and onions to a separate platter. Take out the bay leaves, thyme, and parsley and toss 'em.

- Add the mushrooms to the broth and heat on high. Keep up the heat until it reduces by about three-fourths and it becomes thick and saucy. Lower the heat, stir in the butter, and return the chicken and the onions to the Dutch oven. Coat the chicken and onions, and add more seasoning if necessary.

- Garnish with the parsley and serve with Don Giovanni.

# THE CASE OF THE FOWL PREDICTION
*Where we learn the difference between chickens and pigeons*

I checked in with my message service this morning because, deep down, despite what people might say, I'm an optimist at heart. In fact, I consider it an act of optimism just to have a message service. The young gum-chewer who manned my line, as well as the hundreds of other optimists they charged by the month, surprised me with a message that wasn't an invitation to purchase encyclopedias or an inquiry as to whether or not my icebox was running.

"You've got a message from someone calling themselves 'Calabash' or something like that," she said, paying more attention to her nails than to me.

"I don't suppose that you managed to pry a return phone number out of the stiff?" I asked, my optimism in full recession.

"No, smart guy," answered the charm school candidate, filing what must have been the remnants of her last customer away from her fingernails. "He didn't leave no phone number. He left an address though, and said that you should hot foot it over there as soon as you could."

The card she handed me had the words "Mr. Cala-something" scribbled at the top, and an address on Adams Street that I could make out if I squinted hard. I thanked her and tossed her a two-bit tip. For a minute, I thought that she might toss it back.

"Thanks a lot, big spender," she grumbled, dropping the quarter onto the desk and returning to her manicure. I threw a nod back at her and went on my way, feeling a little less optimistic than when I came in.

265 Adams Street was an unfamiliar neighborhood to me, and after spending two seconds there, I could tell why. The homes of Adams Street were ivy-covered, picket fence affairs that my Aunt Petunia would have described as 'quaint.' Each little plot of heaven had a postage-stamp sized lawn in front and window boxes that overflowed with begonias or gardenias, or whatever it was that grew in the suburbs. It was a colony of trimmed hedges and clean streets that rubbed shoulders against the sleeping giant of the city. Looking at the front yard, I was surprised that the colonists hadn't lynched whoever lived here.

I opened the gate to the Adams Street house, and was immediately mobbed by an aggressive bunch of chickens intent on drawing blood.

My shins and toes were assaulted by the pecking and scratching of this malevolent brood, but I managed to keep a bit of my dignity and shooed some of the foul creatures away. All but one.

The lead chicken was a large, plump, bully of an old hen with a plume of dark feathers around her neck and malice in her heart. She picked up where the others left off, charged at me with a fire in her eyes that I hadn't seen equaled in even the cruelest mob bosses. She was relentless, and I considered punting the hen over the picket fence as if she were pigskin. Before I could take a decent backswing, however, the front door opened, and a familiar voice rang out.

"Lulu, behave yourself!" Since no one had referred to me as "Lulu" since the third grade, I assumed that the voice was calling out to the chicken. I followed the voice, and was surprised to find a familiar face attached.

"Miguel Ramirez?" I asked. I could not have been more surprised if the chicken had called out. Miguel Ramirez was a small time operator from my old neighborhood and the two of us used to run numbers for his uncle at the corner bar. A war broke out during our last year at reform school, we were just young and idealistic enough to join up the day we graduated. Or in Miguel's case, should have graduated. I went off to war and was shipped overseas. Miguel stayed home and learned the fine art of flimflam.

The man who stood in front of me still had the face of the kid I knew from the neighborhood, but had grown at least a foot since then, and weighed even less than when I last saw him. He was a tall, dark figure, with jet black hair pulled into a long pony tail. Evidently he hadn't seen a barber since we had parted. He sauntered up to me as if the world had laid out a red carpet just for him.

"Miguel, you look great," I said, "but there has to be some kind of mistake. I'm here to see a man by the name of 'Cavendish.'" He almost doubled over in laughter.

"It's Kandu!" he said. "I told the young woman that you were to come here to meet "Kandu the Mysterious.""

I looked at Miguel's goofy grin as he waited for me to catch up. If there was a joke to be had, I was missing it.

"So you're 'Kandu!'" I said to Miguel's widening smile. I really was going to have to get a better message service. I shook my head as a tiny, dim bulb went on over my head. "All right, what's your racket?"

"I am Kandu the Mysterious, all-seeing and all-knowing. Allow me to be your spirit guide into the realms of the unknown, where all will reveal itself to your humble servant in perfect clarity." He closed his eyes and raised his upturned palms as he spoke, and my hand instinctively checked my wallet.

"Did you ever stop to consider for a moment that there might actually be a hell for liars?" I told the fake fakir. When he opened his eyes again, the boyish grin returned.

"I can't imagine any higher being finding me anything less than charming," he said, and if that higher power were anything like the girls in our old neighborhood, Miguel had no worries.

"In that case, the higher power better guard his billfold. How long have you been running this racket?"

"You wound me," said Miguel, with well-practiced sincerity. "I've been drawn to the existential my entire life, but let's be civilized and have a snoot before business. Lulu, down honey!" The evil hen managed to get in a couple more pecks before I shooed her away. I closed the door quickly before the fowl followed me inside, and was surprised to find myself smack-dab in the middle of a posh parlor, complete with red satin curtains, matching rug, chandelier, and a small, round table covered with a heavy tablecloth. In the center of the table was a large crystal ball, resting on a brass holder. The room was intimate, but I had no doubt that there was much more than met the eye.

"Please allow me to welcome you to my humble parlor," said Miguel as he pulled a chair out for me. I sat down and Miguel reached behind a nearby curtain and produced, as if by magic, a small bottle and a couple of shot glasses. He poured a couple of fingers into each glass, and we toasted our alma mater, the School of Hard Knocks.

"Now look, Miguel," I said, getting down to brass tacks. "It isn't like old-home week isn't swell and all, but how's about running down this little scam for me?"

"It's like this," said the charming con man. "The society swells meet me at a cocktail party or fund raiser, and I dazzle them with a little of the old 'pulling back the celestial veil.' Just a taste you, understand. Then I give them a card, have them stop by here, and give them a full reading."

"And the show begins," I sighed.

"Exactly! And once they get a bit of the song and dance, voila! They're hooked! Repeat customers!"

"And the song and dance is…?" I asked. I barely saw him so much as twitch as the lights in the parlor went out. I felt a breeze blow through the room, and I heard music in the distance. An eerie light filled the celling, and a brass trombone appeared to be floating over our table. Our table rose and tilted, even though both of Miguel's hands rested on the top. After a moment of this, the lights came back on, and all appeared as it was before.

"Not bad," I said, honestly impressed with the display. "Can you pull a rabbit from your hat as well?"

"That stuff's for suckers," he told me, the pride brimming over in his voice. "I'm strictly first class all the way."

I held a hand up to cut him off before whatever he was selling started to run downhill. "You can count me out of this racket," I told Miguel. "I'm strictly legit."

"You got it all wrong," Miguel said, shaking his head. "I'm in love."

We retired to the kitchen, bringing the bottle of booze with us to keep the conversation well-lubricated, and Miguel told me about the apple of his felonious eye. Young Kate Worthington came from old-school money and spent her life behind the gilded walls of privilege. She had been raised by nannies and shipped off to boarding school when she was old enough to start being inconvenient. Now of age and coming into her fortune, young Kate was a beautiful young thing with all the world experience of a hot house orchid.

Miguel had first laid eyes on the young debutante when he was running a scam on the partners in Daddy Worthington's law firm. He found his way to becoming the pet sooth-sayer for the senior partner, but while young Miss Worthington was on a break from college, Miguel met her and fell head over heels.

"It's that old story," Miguel said, sipping his whiskey as we watched the chickens scratch in the yard. "I took one look, and it was like the rest of the world didn't exist." He put down his glass and turned towards me, away from the chicken infestation outside.

"I'm a changed man," he said. "I want to marry Kate and she wants to marry me. I bought this house out here so that we could settle down and raise a few kids."

"And you outfitted your new home with fake ghosts and rising tables because…?"

"It's my old life!" he said, throwing his arm towards the front parlor. "I would give it all up today if we could get married."

"As far as I can tell, neither one of you is a child. Why don't you just tell the old man to stuff it, marry little Miss Ivy League, and raise a brood of ill-mannered chickens?"

"Because Jasper Worthington has me under his thumb," he said. "It ain't a stretch to say that I've made some mistakes in my life. I've got a prison record, I'm on parole, and old Jasper could get me sent back up the river with a single phone call.

"And he hasn't done so yet because…?"

"Because Kate and I have kept our love a secret," he said. Myself, I didn't think that people spoke that way anymore, but here we were. "We've lived our lives in the shadows, afraid of what her old man could do. You gotta help me."

"And how can I possibly help you?" I asked. A memory flashed through my head, when I was overseas and my unit found itself smack in the middle of a mine field. The feeling was very similar to how I felt right now.

"I need to get something on the Worthington family," he said. "I need some insurance so that Kate and I can start our lives."

I left Miguel in the front yard, standing among his evil little birds. I promised him that I would at least look into the Worthingtons, and I received a few more pecks and scratches from Miguel's nasty chickens for my trouble. "I can't pay you much," Miguel told me as I closed the gate on the picket fence behind me, "but I'll make you a batch of my mom's beef stew when you're done." I told him where he could stick the beef stew and went to work.

I did some light digging on the Worthington family and found that they had indeed battened down their family hatches. What the world at large knew about them was what was printed in the society pages. Daddy Warbucks Worthington was a pillar in the community. Mrs. Worthington took the silver spoon out of her mouth on weekends and used it in a soup kitchen on the East Side. If they had any skeletons in their closet, the closet was padlocked, boarded, and guarded by pit-bulls. Kate, on the other hand, was what we in the trade referred to as colorful.

Little Kate was an only child, and her parents would only have dipped her baby shoes in bronze if they could dip them in gold first. If there was anything she was left wanting for as a child, I couldn't find it. The parade of nannies, wet nurses, tutors, and baby sitters that made up most of Kate's young life read like the cast of a Cecil B. DeMille movie. I could have asked Miguel to give me the rundown on young Kate's life, but I wouldn't trust him if he told me the correct color of smog.

After calling in a favor or two at the DA's office, I found that young Kate had never been convicted or arrested, but it wasn't due to lack of trying. My contact, Mike McCarthy, remembered her name right off the top of his head, which was never a good sign. He told me that Kate Worthington spent both money and time like it was going out of style, and made a habit of paying no attention whatsoever to the rules that might slow her down. Everything from jaywalking to narcotics laws were bent or broken, and Kate's father employed a junior partner in the firm just so he could clean up her nights on the town. It also looked as if the junior partner worked overtime. Miguel had described Kate Worthington with violins and rainbows, but the picture I had of her was hot jazz and bathtub hooch. And that meant there was more to this than met the eye.

I changed gears by staking out Kate's apartment. I waited for her to start her evening, and was a little surprised that her evening started around ten. As Kate sped off in a little convertible that was specially equipped to drive on the sidewalks, I hailed a cab to tail her. I had to hand over an extra C-note to the cabbie just so he could keep up. The cabbie, to his credit, managed to keep her taillights in sight, and we tailed her to the Pretty Kitty Night Club.

The Kitty had a strict clientele policy that was intended to keep out mugs like me. It was the hallmark of a nice club, and I was sure that there was a photo of me hanging up in the coatroom, just in case. In most circumstances, I would have handed the chimp working the door a C-note and chalked it up to my client's expenses. In this case, the expenses went to Miguel, and I was sure that payment would not be forthcoming. I was afraid that I might just have to dig into my own pocket to gain entrance, but then Lady Luck decided not to spit in my face for once and I caught a break.

This particular door monkey was one Paulie the Pick, and even though he cut a fine figure as an impassable obstacle on the door, he owed me one from a few months earlier, when I provided him with an alibi for a stabbing in the East End. The big lug was losing money to me in a poker game, but when your nickname is "the Pick," cops generally look to you first whenever they find a mug that is, shall we say, perforated.

"Hey, shamus," said Paulie as I approached the big lug. He grinned, showing off a selection of broken and missing teeth that reminded me that one didn't get the position of working the door by hitting the books.

"Hey yourself, handsome," I said, stepping in front of the swells who were waiting in line for entrance to the Kitty. They were well-dressed society stiffs who made enough to wait in line, but not enough to get to the head of it. The couple I stepped in front of probably spent the last half-hour waiting in line before I cut them off, and they looked a little put-out. The guy started to protest to Paulie, but zipped it up pretty quickly when the Pick snapped open a switchblade and began to clean his nails.

"So what can I do for a pal?" he asked as nonchalantly as a man picking his nails with a switchblade could.

"I was hoping for an invite," I told Paulie. "I'm trying to meet a better class of people."

"Well, they're richer in there," said Paulie, not bothering to look up, "but I wouldn't call them better. Heck, I've seen kinder souls doing hard time."

"Still, I imagine it pays the bills," I told Paulie, and he nodded, spiriting his switchblade away and cracking open the door for me to enter. From inside, jazz and cigarette smoke spilled out to the hopefuls waiting in line.

"I imagine that's what you're doing here," said Paulie. I nodded and said that I was working on a favor for another friend. If I still believed the story that Miguel handed me, then young Kate was as fragile as a lily in springtime. If she was a regular here, then Paulie would know.

"I'm looking for a dame," I told the Pick, flashing a photo I had dug up from the Society page.

"So's every other Romeo in this joint," laughed Paulie. He took a look at the newspaper clipping I flashed and gave a long whistle. "Her?" Paulie shook his head. "You're gonna have your hands full with this one, gumshoe." Paulie had been around the block more times than an ice cream truck, and when a guy like the Pick whistled, it wasn't because he forgot the lyrics.

"You know the story on this dame?" I asked Paulie.

"On 'Good Time Katie?'" laughed Paulie. "Only that you can find her in her usual corner, holding court by draining her trust fund as fast as she can." He threw a nod towards the bar. About a half dozen young men with their gears stuck in high surrounded a barstool. I could only guess that somewhere in the middle of the mass of young men was "Good Time Katie." I patted Paulie on the back and made my way over to the sea of eager fellows. On my way through the crowded club, I drew more than a few stares that led me to think my tie might have clashed with my jacket. I got to the boys surrounding the good Miss Worthington, took a deep breath, and waded in.

"Do you mind?" asked one of the young men as I jostled my way through the crowd. I smiled and opened my jacket, letting the young man lay eyes on the snub nose in my shoulder holster. The crowd thinned.

"Well, do I know you?" slurred a kitten in a full length evening gown. She had raven hair, ruby lips, and the smell of gin was so thick on her breath I was surprised the wallpaper adhered to the walls.

"Sure you do, kid," I said, putting a heavy hand on the shoulder of her last remaining would-be suitor. The kid got the message and high-tailed it back to the bar. Kate fished around in her pocketbook and came up with a cigarette. She also managed to come up with a lighter but, after a few tries, the task of lighting it proved too much. I took the lighter and lit her cigarette for her. I find it's the little things that help build trust.

"I saw the gun," she said, cutting right to the heart of the matter. "Are you a cop?"

"I'm a private detective," I told her. "I was asked to look in and make sure that no one is disgracing the family name."

"Who would do that?" she slurred, throwing her arms open and scaring off her neighbors with a lit cigarette. Despite the law of gravity, the delicate flower wobbled in her bar stool but stayed upright. "The only thing that could make this night better was if you wouldn't let me drink by myself." I looked at the sea of men waiting to take my seat as soon as I vacated it, and thought she wasn't a woman destined to be alone for long.

As if by magic, a champagne flute appeared on the table in front of me, and young Kate filled it for me, emptying the bottle in the process. Without looking she dropped the bottle behind her, where it landed on a pile of its dead confederates. Kate took a drag of her cigarette, and motioned to a waiter at the same time. From somewhere under the table I felt a hand grip my thigh.

I hoped it was Kate, but no matter who it was, it wasn't good.

"I'm here on behalf of a friend," I told Kate, prying her fingers from my leg. "He's concerned that you might be getting yourself into trouble." If this was the woman that Miguel had fallen in love with, it was he who was looking for trouble.

"So you're sorta like Cyrano Dewatsis?" she said, draining her glass to make room for the limited amount of bubbly that wasn't already inside her.

"Er, yeah, exactly like that," I said. Something wasn't adding up. The woman across the table from me, the one with the wooden leg, didn't jibe with the innocent kid that Miguel described to me. Miguel just wasn't that naive. I sipped my champagne as she gulped hers, asked a few more questions, and listened to the musical stylings of one of the Dorsey brothers.

Kate Worthington told me her life's story, a story mostly punctuated with men. As she went into detail about her years abroad, I lost count of the loves of her life, but that was probably my fault. I only had ten fingers.

"I'm sure it's been a full and rich journey," I told young Kate, "But where does Miguel come in?"

"Who?" Kate asked, her eyelids beginning to sag.

"Miguel Ramirez," I told the young drunk. "Tall, dark and weighs about one fifty nothing?" The alcohol haze continued to cloud her eyes. She still had no idea what I was talking about.

"Dark hair, dark eyes, and equally dark heart?" I asked. "He knows all, tells all? Has a way with a crystal ball?" I still saw no recollection. "Your boyfriend?"

"Oh, Kandu!" she said with a squeal. "He's absolutely yummy!" Her appearance took a conspiratorial look, and for the briefest of moments, she might have passed for sober.

"He's my spiritual advisor," she slurred. "I don't make a move without him."

"So you're not his girlfriend?" I asked.

"Girlfriend?" she said with a gasp that expelled a small cloud of champagne. "For God's sake, the man is a fortune teller! I wouldn't date a fortune teller any more than I would..."

"A private eye?" I suggested.

"Exactly!" replied Kate. "It would be like dating the town drunk!" I looked down to see that Kate had drained her latest flute of bubbly. I decided to let the town drunk crack pass.

"Besides," she said, motioning for the river of champagne to flow once again. "Daddy would cut me off if I were to take up with someone so ..."

"Interesting?" I suggested.

"Pedestrian," she said.

"Perish the thought," I said, rising from the table. My chair hadn't even cooled before another able young body filled it. I gave a wave to Kate, but she was too busy drinking in her next companion.

I left the Pretty Kitty Night Club and grabbed a cab. Here in the well-lit, well-monied streets of uptown, cabs were easy to get. When I told the cabbie where I wanted to go, he seemed disappointed. Once he got to the suburbs, there were no more fares to be had. While the cabbie drove, I had time to sit back and add up what Katie and Miguel had told me. The math didn't work, but I had time, the road, and a tight-lipped cabbie in my favor, so by the time I got to Miguel's house I was able to fudge the equations.

I let myself into the yard, where the hen lay in wait. She attacked my shins in earnest, but this time I wasn't in the mood. I already had a few bandages on my calves from our earlier meeting and this time I was ready for little Lulu. I took care of the pugnacious bird and rang Miguel's doorbell.

"Ah, my friend, come in," said Miguel, bowing and bidding me welcome with a wave of his hand. I sat down at the same round table that the spirits levitated earlier. Miguel turned his back and dug the booze bottle and glasses out of his hidey-hole and poured us a couple of drinks. We clinked our glasses together once again and drank.

"I have awaited your return with bated breath. So what were you able to find out about my beloved?"

"I found out that Kate can drink any sailor in the fleet under the table, she has absolutely no sense of sarcasm, and that her fiancé is a no good, lying, piece of...."

"Easy, there gumshoe," said Miguel, holding up his hands in defense. "I can hear you, after all."

"Maybe, but you aren't her boyfriend." I said, tossing back the last of the booze. "She doesn't even have one."

"What makes you say that, hombre?"

"Because I have a brain in my head and occasionally I use it."

Miguel had been running the Kandu scam in town for a while, but there was only so much info a false fakir could divine using luck, charm, or cheap booze, and in the mystical world of the here-after, inside information was the coin of the realm. He had used his skill to find out what he could about his mark, hook them on his fortune-telling grift, and then reel them into his parlor. Once there, Dear Uncle Whatziz would speak to the mark through Miguel, and the spirits would instruct the bereaved to start writing checks. When the information stopped, Kandu would skip town.

Miguel had run his scam for a while now, making it tick with clockwork precision. He was on the verge of blowing town when he met Kate Worthington and her all-star trust fund. She was too good to pass up, but he had already been running the Kandu grift thin and had to blow before his past caught up to him. In order to do this and reel in Kate, he needed to dig up everything he could on her in a jiffy. That was where I came in.

"And I'm not giving you anything," I told the smarmy conman.

"Beg your pardon?" asked Miguel, pausing in mid-pour.

"I'm not going to let you get one over on this kid," I said, taking the shot glass and downing what was there before the grifter had a chance to pour it back in the bottle. "I'm not going to help you run your scam on the Worthington girl so that you can wad up a towel on your head and milk her for her fortune."

"It is called a turban, you cut-rate gumshoe," Miguel hissed at me. He quickly grabbed the shot glass from my hand and tossed it to the floor, shattering it into pieces. "And Kate Worthington is no saint! When did you become a boy scout?"

"Not a boy scout," I told him. "I just feel for the little moron. I would rather see her throw away her fortune the old fashioned way than see you scam it out from under her."

"Fine," said Miguel, smoothing his jacket and opening his door for me. I turned and walked through his yard. He followed me out. "Just remember we used to be friends. That's over!"

I turned quickly and fixed Miguel hard in the eye. He stepped back, half expecting me to paste him one.

"That's hardly the Kandu attitude," I said, tipping my hat and stepping through the gate. I locked it behind me and walked down the street. Behind me I could hear Miguel calling for Lulu.

It seemed that his fortunes, as well as his hen, had escaped him.

# GRIFTER'S TACOS DE POLLO

2 lbs. boneless, skinless chicken thighs, diced

1/3 cup olive oil

2 tablespoons tequila

2 cloves garlic (minced)

1 small minced onion

1 tablespoon paprika

1 teaspoon chili powder

1 teaspoon salt

3 tablespoons cilantro

Corn tortillas

1 cup Queso Blanco, shredded

- Put the first nine ingredients in a bowl and park it overnight in the icebox. The next day pull the bowl out and let it rest until it reaches room temperature, about ten minutes.

- Heat a skillet over medium heat and spread out the chicken in the skillet, stirring well and heating until well cooked.

- Spoon the chicken over a couple of warm tortillas, top with the shredded cheese, and enjoy them in a peaceful, hen-free environment.

# THE CASE OF THE HIGH STEAKS
*Where a young detective is both seasoned and tenderized*

I closed my office door behind me carefully and turned off the lights as I made my way to my desk as best I could. I put down the package I had gotten on my way over and tore open the butcher's paper and twine that bound it. Inside was one of the leanest, trimmest, well-marbled prime cuts of beef that had ever graced Milton's Butcher Shop around the corner. I gazed at it briefly in awe before I leaned my head backwards and slapped the steak on my swelling, discolored eye.

Earlier in the week I had taken the case of one Delores Melrose. Delores' husband Earl owned the largest and most successful sporting goods shop in the city, creatively named Melrose Sports. According to Delores, Earl spent around fifty hours a week turning the once small mom-and-pop into a thriving purveyor of jump ropes and dumbbells. At least that was the story he was peddling to Delores.

In reality, Earl was giving his cardio-pulmonary system a brisk workout with his young, blonde secretary. The secretary in question, one Eloise Johnson, had been employed at Melrose Sports for well over three months and, unless pictures did lie, was quite a specimen herself. Delores suspected that the buxom Miss Johnson, whom Earl appeared to replace every three months with an equally buxom Miss Johnson, was having a little bit of something with her husband Earl.

Delores had given me a laundry list of Earl's favorite hideaways, and the amount of detail she put into the list was staggering. So much detail that it caused me to question exactly how Delores had landed the big, muscular fish in the first place. Delores wasn't paying me to speculate on her sporting pursuits, so I let them be and focused on her husband and Miss Johnson. Delores had laid out where he liked to eat, his favorite watering holes, and even the night clubs he might happen to frequent during the odd business trips. She gave me all the information the intrepid investigator might need to snap a few pictures of her husband and his secretary taking some informal dictation. Delores provided me with every bit of information on her husband that I might need to wrap up this case but one.

She didn't tell me that Earl had been a Golden Gloves Champ in his Navy days.

The steak still felt cool on my eye, and I let out a long breath. After Earl had mopped up the floor with yours truly, his wife Delores had entered stage right and had it out with Miss Johnson, handing the young blonde her pink slip along with a handful of dyed roots in the way of severance. Eloise saw the better part of valor and got out while the getting was good, leaving Earl and Delores to have it out while I spent some quality time giving the sidewalk close inspection. The pair fought like cats and dogs before quickly and rather passionately making up. They stepped over my prone body as they made their way home, arm in arm, sharing laughter and forgiveness.

At least that's how the beat cop who woke me up described the situation. From there I made it to the butcher's shop, forked over a few bucks for medicinal steak, and made my way to my office. When I examined my eye in the mirror, I made a mental note to add the cost of the steak to my bill, and hope that it wasn't Mr. Melrose opening the mail that day.

I laid my aching head on my office couch and watched the shadows grow long. That's the way it looked through my one good eye. After a while the aspirin kicked in and my head settled into a more manageable throbbing. I settled down into a long and well-deserved sleep.

A knock on my door came, right on cue.

"Go away," I told the heavy knuckles. The words pounded in my head almost as much as the knocking.

"I'm looking for a detective," said a distinctly feminine voice. It was the kind of throaty, seductive voice that meant doom for guys like me, but usually the kind of doom they went to with a grin from ear to ear.

"He's retired," I groaned. "He opened up a bar on the beach in Key West. The kind that serves drinks with those little umbrellas." The kind of place where detectives do not get routinely punched in the face,

I mumbled to myself. I heard the creak of the door and sighed. Guys who don't lock the doors to their office when they lie down probably deserve to get punched in the face.

"Are you all right?" asked the throaty voice. I opened my one good eye to see a pair of very expensive pair of high heels. The heels were attached to a pair of legs that went on for as long as my good eye could see. The whole package was enough to make me sit up and take notice.

"Couldn't be better," I said as I tossed the steak into the wrapper that sat on my desk and swept the whole package into my top drawer, right on top of my revolver. I stepped over to the guest side of my desk and pulled out a chair for the lady. She sat and I took my seat opposite her behind my desk. She was a red-headed knockout, wearing a tight baby-blue dress that did its level best to keep up with her. I asked her how I could help her and hoped that she took my staring to mean that I was a particularly observant sleuth.

"That's quite an eye you're sporting," said Throaty, nodding her head towards my shiner.

"This old thing? It's nothing," I countered, opening a pad of paper in the pretense of professionalism. "Cut myself shaving this morning. What can I do for you?"

The red-head told me her name was Wanda Tate, and that she was the daughter of a Dr. Martin Tate, a well-known researcher and inventor. I had never heard of either of them and I suspected that well-known researchers and inventors didn't really exist. Since it's bad business to call clients liars to their faces, I pretended to write all this down. Besides, with my luck, she just might belt me one.

"Dear old dad sounds swell," I said. "Where do I come in?"

"I'm here because dad disappeared last night. This morning I found his laboratory in disarray. Equipment had been smashed, files were rifled through, and the desk drawers were pulled out and smashed to pieces." I assumed that all this wasn't a bad housekeeping day and that someone had given the lab a 'once over.'

"And you think that someone made off with the old man?"

"I don't know," said Wanda as tears began to seep from her forest green eyes and made their way down the labyrinth of freckles that dotted her cheeks. I knew in that very moment that I would be taking her case, because I'm that kind of stupid. "I don't have anyone to turn to…."

I gave Wanda Tate the standard "chin up" speech that all detectives hand to their weeping clients. I think it came from a dime-store comic book. I told Wanda that it was hopeful that there hadn't been any note or mention of ransom. I had no idea if this was true, but it sounded good. You should never tell a client that you don't have a clue as to how to proceed on a case. Page fifteen of the handbook is very clear on this.

My client told me that she had spoken to the police shortly after she left her father's lab. The police did their due diligence, patiently listening, filling out a report, and efficiently filing it. I appreciated the effort on Wanda's part. It saved me the time and effort of visiting the precinct house and having the cops make fun of me.

I told her that I would give Pop Tate's lab and office the once over and poke around as to his whereabouts. I wished her a good night before I took my steak out of my office drawer and properly wrapped it up. I made a brief stop at my apartment to toss the steak into my icebox before I checked the local hospitals and morgues. That's page eighty-seven of the handbook. Never tell clients that you are looking in the morgue for their loved ones.

I came up snake eyes with the hospitals and morgue, so I headed to the lab and it was every bit as bad as reported. There were shards of beakers, test tubes, and science whatsis all over the place, and the good doctor's files took up whatever space on the floor the equipment missed. The couch cushions had been torn open and ripped apart, the file cabinets pulled away from the walls, and the vents had been removed. It wasn't an amateur job. Someone had given the place a methodical going over, and it looked as if they had come up short. Since I couldn't do any more damage to this dump, I made the trek uptown to Tate's apartment.

The Tate residence was in similar condition, drawers pulled out and cabinets thrown this way and that, but the closets were bare and the suitcases were gone. A quick check revealed that the doctor's toothbrush, shaving kit, and most of his personal possessions had disappeared as well. The only thing left were some pictures on his desk of him on the college swim team and of him on a sailboat. Everything else was either broken or gone.

I spoke to a few of his neighbors, at least those who were willing to answer questions from a guy sporting a shiner. They told me that the doctor had kept to himself and they had only known him well enough for the odd 'hello' and 'goodbye.' They told me that they had heard a racket coming from his place the other night, but when I asked if anyone called the cops, they looked at me as if I were trying to convert them to religion. I asked if they recalled meeting the doctor's daughter, but my dime had apparently run out because the door slammed in my face.

All in all, it looked as if I had struck out without swinging. I decided to call it a night.


It rained on the way, because it always rains when detectives walk to their office at night. See page eighty-one. By the time I got their I was drenched, tired, hungry, and my eye throbbed. I was beginning to think that my mother was right. Maybe orthodontia WAS the way to go. I took out my key and started to open my door and then I froze.

I keep a small piece of thread draped over the top of my door whenever I leave my apartment. I do this so that when I get back I can tell if someone has let themselves in during my absence. And before you ask, this was page seventy-three, but in the Scout's Handbook. I let out a breath, drew my revolver from my shoulder holster, slid my key silently into the lock, and prepared to greet my guest.

I threw open the door and aimed my gun with one hand while I flipped on the lights with the other. Caught like deer in headlights were two palookas in the process of redecorating my office in the same style that had graced Doctor Tate's place.

Both apes wore dark suits with long coats and fedoras. The one furthest from me, the younger of the two, was in the middle of going through my desk and looked like a disobedient kid who had just got caught with his hand in the cookie jar. The other mug was going through my files, and from his language I figured he must have spent some time in the navy. I waved the gun towards the ceiling and they reached for it.

"I appreciate the hard work, boys," I told them as I waved them towards the far corner of the small office, "but I was hoping for a colonial décor." I reached for the phone, keeping one eye as well as my gun pointed at my guests. I started to call for the cops when one of the monkeys found his voice.

"I wouldn't do that if I were you," said the lead ape, the one who had cursed when I opened the door.

"I hope you weren't planning on an evening of ghost stories and hair braiding."

"We're feds," said the palooka. I looked at the other mug, but he was still staring at his shoes, looking like a puppy that just got the business end of a newspaper.

"Okay, big guy," I told the lead palooka. "Prove it. But go nice and slow." He started to reach into his lapel before I stopped him. "Only two fingers better go inside that lapel, or none are coming out."

He slowly reached into his jacket and brought out a wallet, holding it between his thumb and index finger. Looking at me for permission, he opened it up to show me his credentials.

"Is that good enough, tough guy?" he asked me. I told him to hand me his wallet so I could have a look, and I examined his ID as if I could tell if it were a forgery. It wasn't issued by Ovaltine, so I gave it back to him and lowered my gun.

"G-Men," I said with disgust. "Do you feds usually make it a habit of going through honest folk's property?"

"Honest folk, no," said Agent Whoever, obviously the leader of the duo. "Mugs like you are fairer game than most." Behind him, the younger agent was looking at me through narrow eyes, obviously in an attempt to let me know that J. Edgar's boys didn't like to be trifled with. His face was still red with anger and his freckles glowed. I resisted the urge to tousle his hair and dealt with his boss.

"So what is it you're looking for?" I asked. "And please answer my question before I ask either of you goons to show me some kind of warrant." The ring leader gritted his teeth a moment and sighed.

"We're looking for some papers regarding a… detection device," said the big guy. The kid continued to try and burn holes through me with his eyes. "We've got the inventor of the dingus on ice, and most of his papers as well, but there are a few items that we need to run down."

"I put two and two together, and the result comes up 'classified.' You've got most of old Doc Tate's plans for a secret radar doohickey, and the old man himself, but the old boy can't remember some of his mojo and you thought I might have it." I watched the junior G-men's mouths drop open. There's nothing like getting one over on the feds to make a gumshoe feel superior. When the boys composed themselves, their eyes told me that I might be put on ice right next to Doc Tate. I held up my hands in defense.

"I might happen to know which Cracker Jack box the prize is in, but you gotta fill me in on a little of the good doctor's family life." The younger fed looked as if he wanted to introduce me to his handcuffs, but his boss' cooler head prevailed.

"Uncle Sam doesn't make a habit of playing ball with small time operators like yourself," said the senior agent.

"Yeah, Uncle Sam does have that reputation. But if you CAN find it in your heart to play ball with me, I think I can put a bow on all this for you."

The senior agent sighed and nodded to his partner. Junior closed the drawer he had been rummaging through and Senior pulled out a chair and sat down. I walked over to the hotplate, put on some water for coffee, and we settled down for a nice little chat.

I called the number that Wanda had given me and told her to meet me at my office that evening at seven. I gave her the good news that I had found Daddy Dearest and all the information was wrapped up in a dossier for her, available to her as soon as she paid my fee. The bad news for her was that the fee had ballooned up a bit, to around two grand. She balked in that throaty voice I had grown so fond of, but eventually she agreed to meet me at seven.

Around six-fifteen I heard a rattling of my office doorknob, followed by the gentle clicking of the lock. The door eased open a crack, and the barrel of a revolver snuck through the opening. The chair behind my desk faced towards the window, as if I were watching the rain. A shot rang out, the bullet hitting the hat that peeked over the top of my chair.

The bullet found a home in the stack of books that sat on my chair, keeping the hat aloft.

"Federal Agents!" barked the boys, rushing in from the office across the hall behind the lovely Miss Tate. The senior agent liberated the pistol from her hand as Junior pulled her hands together and accessorized her pearl necklace with a pair of Uncle Sam's finest steel bracelets.

"What is going on?" gasped the lovely Wanda as she was wrapped up by our nation's finest. "How dare you…?"

"Lock you up for trying to kill yours truly?" I asked, walking behind my desk to retrieve my hat. I held the hat in front of my face and looked through the hole in the crown. While it wouldn't work for winter, it was freshly air conditioned for spring.

"It started when I went looking for your 'father.' I went through his lab, his papers, his apartment, and I couldn't find a hint as to who made off with the old boy. It wasn't until I met up with the men from Good Humor here in my office that I finally discovered that the feds had swooped in and whisked the good doctor off to an undisclosed location."

"Do you really have to explain all this?" snarled the senior agent as he force-fed the woman I knew as Wanda Tate her rights. From the way she was dragging her feet and the European curse words flying from her mouth, I didn't think that she was interested in remaining silent.

"I only want my moment in the sun," I told the G-man. "Besides I have to tell 'Wanda' here how I figured out that she wasn't the good Doctor's daughter."

"Fine," said Dick Tracy. "Just make it snappy!"

"It was the doctor's desk in the lab that first clued me in," I told the woman as she threw a kick towards the shin of the young civil servant. "He had no pictures of a wife or kids. The only sentimental thing there was an autographed picture of Pee Wee Reese."

"Could you wrap this up?" asked the fed, wrestling with the tiger. "Then, in his apartment, he had pictures of vacations and graduations, but nothing to let me believe that he had ever had a family, let alone a loving and concerned daughter." I moved in closer to the hellcat so that I didn't have to gloat from a distance.

"By the time I met the boys here in my apartment, I knew that my client, like most of my clients, had lied to me." I put a finger to her chin and tilted her head upwards, so that our eyes locked. "Unlike most of my clients, though, you were a foreign spy, out looking for the radar system that the good doctor was working on."

I caught a brief smile from Wanda that confirmed my story, and for a moment, I had that rare feeling of satisfaction one gets from outwitting a brilliant opponent.

Then she head-butted me in my one good eye.

After the boys had wrestled Wanda into the wagon, and had a good chuckle about my two black eyes, they gave me a half-hearted, laugh-riddled thank you on behalf of a grateful government as well as a lift home.

And along the way, they stopped at the butcher's shop to get a steak for my other eye.

# GUMSHOE'S NEW YORK STRIP STEAK WITH BASIL

# GARLIC BUTTER

½ lb. New York Strip Steak

¼ cup softened butter

2 tablespoons fresh basil, minced

2 cloves garlic, minced

½ teaspoon of Dijon mustard

¼ paprika

Dash of fresh cracked black pepper

- Let the butter sit out so that it is as soft as an uptown mouthpiece. By hand, blend in the basil, garlic, mustard, paprika, and pepper. Spoon the mixture onto a 12" square of plastic wrap and roll it into a log about 1 ½" in diameter, or approximately the size of hefty lead pipe. Wrap the log in tin foil and put it on ice. You can do this a day or two in advance of cooking your steak.

- For the steak, remove it from the refrigerator about fifteen minutes ahead of cooking time and let it come to room temperature. Preheat your oven to 350 F and put a good old-fashioned cast iron skillet over high heat. Sear both sides of the steak, giving them a good char, and shove the whole thing, skillet and all, into the oven. Continue to cook until the temperature inside the steak is a delicious 145 F.

- Remove the steak from the oven and allow it to rest about ten minutes. Place a slice of your buttery garlicky goodness on top and enjoy the sight through swollen, squinty eyes.

# THE CASE OF THE UNDERCOVER MULLIGAN
*Where old friends are in the stew*

T he apartments in the East Side, for the most part, lack such modern niceties as garbage disposals, circulating fans, and privacy. I know this first-hand because the racket I was causing would have woken up Ulysses S. Grant from his slumber. I beat on the door like Buddy Rich on his skins, and inside I could hear the banging of pots and pans, as well as the feeble assurances that the man of the house was on his way. The door started to open but it took the hand on the other side a half dozen tries to open it. It was summer in the city, and the wood of the door had swelled to twice its size inside the frame, so I didn't take it as too much of a condemnation that it took the guy inside all his mustard to get the door open.

"Who's there?" asked the occupant through the chained crack in the door. The man inside was a scrawny, bookish young man with the sharp, twig-like features that would have a hard time standing up to a stiff breeze. In between sentences I could hear the whistle of a deviated septum and the wheeze of a body built by a lifetime lifting number two pencils.

"The person you called at four in the morning begging to come down here," I sighed, seeing my beaten expression in the pop bottle glasses through the door. The glasses belonged to Hughie Cranski, a small-time pulp writer who made his way in life at five cents a word, going by the pen name Hugh W. Cranston.

I had known Hughie most of my life, starting in grade school when I had walked into the locker room during Phys Ed and caught the starting line-backer corp dangling him upside down over the commode. I 'convinced' the home team to give Hughie a pass, and ever since then the kid followed me around like a stray.

Hughie squinted through his grimy lenses and whispered through the crack in the door.

"How do I know it's you?" As an answer I flicked him in the forehead.

"That do it for you?" I asked, and he unlatched the door and let me in, rubbing his forehead as he did so.

Hughie's apartment was a Cracker Jack box, making my apartment look like the Taj Mahal by comparison. The hovel was littered with pulp magazines, what looked like rejection letters, and a Charles Atlas mail order course that looked like it hadn't seen much use. The only bit of order in the sea of chaos was Hughie's pride and joy, a Royal Classic typewriter and a fresh ream of typing paper.

"Come in," said Hughie, retreating into his apartment and pointing me in the direction of what looked like a newspaper-upholstered sofa. "Make yourself at home." I would have, but my home was twenty blocks away.

"Hughie," I sighed. "When you called me, you said it was urgent...."

"It IS urgent," said the bookworm, walking to the kitchen and grabbing two small bowls from a shelf. There was a pot on the fire, and I could hear whatever was inside simmering. Whatever was on the fire smelled wonderful, and helped make an otherwise wretched apartment bearable.

"Mulligan Stew," Hughie said, handing me a bowl and a spoon. "Ma Cranski's pride and joy. One single pot fed fourteen screaming children." I started to tell Hughie that I didn't come fifteen blocks out of my way for a midnight snack, but the stew smelled good and Hughie sweetened the deal by pouring a couple fingers of booze into an old peanut butter jar. We sat down, clinked our glasses together and Hughie threw back his drink, because that's what he saw detectives do in the movies. I spent the next ten minutes slapping him on the back as he fought for air. When the color returned to his face, I introduced him to a little four-letter detective jargon regarding wasting one's time in the middle of the night.

"I called you because I'm onto something big and I need you to provide some back-up." Hughie sat up a little straighter and puffed up his chest. Somewhere in the back of my head I felt a headache rolling up its sleeves to get to some serious work.

"I'm in a new line of work," said Hughie, reaching into his breast pocket and producing a business card the way that a magician produces a rabbit from his fedora. The card read 'Hugh W. Cranston, Investigative Reporter.'

"And what exactly is 'Investigative Reporter Hugh W. Cranston' on to?"

"An expose!" shouted Hughie, widening his hands and pointing out the headline of an imaginary newspaper. "Crime! Corruption! Scandal! The seamy underbelly of a thriving, vibrant American Metropolis!"

I had to admit he held my attention.

"And where does the average reader find all the 'seamy underbelly' at these days?" I asked.

"Why, in City Hall, of course!"

My hard-working headache turned into a full-blown migraine.

"No!" I told the kid, grabbing him by his thin lapels. "You stay away from City Hall! If you poke a stick into that beehive, you WILL get stung! Fatally!"

Hughie pushed me off of him with a strength I wouldn't have thought he possessed. Perhaps the Charles Atlas course got some use after all.

City Hall meant Ace Thorndike, the resident worm at the center of the apple. It didn't matter who sat in the Commissioner's, Councilman's or Mayor's seat, they were all there because Ace Thorndike pulled out the chair for them. Whatever deals got dished up at City Hall, be it construction contracts or jay-walking, Ace got a bite. The story that Hughie was after wasn't breaking news. Not in this town. As soon as Ace Thorndike had arrived in this country from parts unknown, he went about taking the city, spreading bribes to any cop with a hand out and taking apart gangs that had the audacity to exist before he made it into this burg. Soon he owned every politician, precinct house, district attorney, and crossing guard in town, and nobody made a move without the official Thorndike stamp of approval.

There was virtually no chance that a newspaper in Timbuktu would run an expose on Ace Thorndike, let alone one in this city. Pursuing this story would only put Hughie in the center of Ace Thorndike's radar, and unlike the high school varsity defense, I couldn't call Thorndike off.

"A lot of people have been looking closely at Thorndike, but so far he's been as slippery as an eel," said Hughie, jumping up and walking to his desk. He dove into the folders he kept on his desk and pulled one up as if it were the Hope Diamond. He brought it back to the couch and flipped it open. "This time is different! I've got the goods on him!"

The folder contained lots of notes on Ace Thorndike, as well as a detailed itinerary of his comings and goings. I would have thought that Thorndike was far too smart to get any dirt on his lily-white hands, but Hughie had pictures of Thorndike leaving the same address on Channel Street every Thursday with a brown paper package tied with string. It all looked perfectly innocent, so I was sure that Hughie could tell me otherwise.

"Okay Hughie, what's in the package?"

"Beats me!" replied Hughie, with the enthusiasm of a kid looking at a chocolate-covered tricycle. "That's where you come in."

"Of course it is."

Hughie laid out his plan to me over another bowl of the Mulligan stew. We were to sneak into Ace Thorndike's office, somewhere beneath the main rock at City Hall, pretending to be cleaners and give his files the once over. Hughie was sure that the smoking gun was hidden there, but I thought that the gun wasn't so much smoking as it was steaming.

"Kid," I said, in that tone I usually reserve for small children and animals before I steal from them. "This is the worst idea I've ever heard. Not only do you NOT stand a chance in hell of getting into Thorndike's office, you stand every chance of getting into a full body cast."

Hughie looked at me as if I'd just slapped him across the face with issue number thirty five of "Exciting Detective Digest."

"Oh," said Hughie. The hero worship drained away from his face and was replaced with a look I was much more accustomed to seeing. "I get it. You're not going to back me up on this one."

"Look kid," I said, feeling like I was about to shed a layer of skin right onto the couch I sat on. "This isn't some kind of cheap, dime-store hood you're looking at. If you go head-to-head with him, he will make you disappear."

"Fine," said Hughie, stomping to the door and throwing it open, letting me know that the endless bowl of stew had indeed reached an end. "Clear out of here. I don't need you anyway if you're yellow."

There was a part of me that wanted to knock the kid into next Tuesday, but there was another part of me that agreed with him.

"Go on," he told me, jerking his thumb towards the hallway beyond the door. "Blow."

So I took his advice and did.

Outside, the wind and the rain beat me as hard as my nagging conscious. I stopped into Gino's Bar and Grill and found Gino reading the comics section and keeping the bar from floating away. I ordered whatever came from the dusty dark bottle that Gino kept under the bar, and then ordered another shot for good measure. It didn't help much. I could still hear Hughie's words in my ears.

Going against Ace Thorndike was like walking head-first into a buzz saw, and I was pretty sure it advised against that in the Private Eye's handbook. Besides, if I were going to continue to do business, I'd need a pulse. Walking away would keep that pulse beating, I just wouldn't feel so proud of it.

"Ya want another shot?" Gino asked automatically. It was the only exercise his lips had beside moving to the hi-jinx of one Mary Worth.

"Naw," I told the barkeep as I flipped up the collar on my trench coat. "I gotta go take a beating."

"Okay," said Gino, moving on to the next comic strip. "You have fun now."

The Thorndike Building was located across the street from City Hall and next to Thorndike Plaza. The address wasn't Thorndike

Boulevard officially, but unofficially, every street in town was. I approached the doorman, who wore a bright, crisp uniform that was so nicely tailored I could barely tell where he hid his gun.

"I'm here to see Ace Thorndike," I told the doorman. He slowly turned towards me and made a face as if he had just bitten into a three-year old donut.

"MISTER Thorndike isn't accepting visitors," he said, maintaining his professional disdain. The implication was that I could take whatever I was selling and beat it, but I was never any good at implications in school, so I held my ground.

"Tell ACE that there is a gentleman down here that has some information on his ocean voyage last August, and some luggage that might have fallen overboard."

The ape in the doorman suit finally gave me his full attention, making a show of looking down about three inches into my eyes. He neither smiled nor blinked, and his look was enough to make me wish I had stayed at Gino's. The name I gave him was "Arthur Conan Doyle," and he took it as if it were last night's garbage.

The truth was I didn't know anything about any "ocean voyage" that Thorndike might or might not have taken, but I knew that Niles the Nose, one of Ace's lieutenants with a nasty gambling problem, had been fished up off the shore late last August. I also knew that Ace had a fleet of yachts in the harbor, and he loved to take his cronies fishing, so I took a shot in the dark, hoping that would be the only one fired tonight.

After a moment or two the doorman returned and led me into an elevator. Inside the elevator was a trained gorilla twice the size of the first orangutan and even more unfriendly, if such a thing were possible. His coat wasn't a tailored job like the doorman's, and it didn't take a Sherlock Holmes to see that he was packing some serious hardware underneath.

The big man kept his own counsel, barely glancing over at me as we rode up to the penthouse floor. I mentioned something about weight-lifting and over-compensating, but he still kept silent. The elevator doors opened and Thorndike's goon nodded his head, urging me out. I walked into the lion's den, and it didn't escape my notice that my shadow got out after me and kept about five paces behind.

The elevator opened into a small hallway with a single door at the end. The mass behind me hung back, so I opened the dark, mahogany door in the middle of what looked like the Urban Malevolent Society.

The room was wall-to-wall bookshelves, with the occasional taxidermied grizzly or suit of armor to break up the monotony. I lost count of oriental rugs covering the paneled floor, and the built-in bar on the far wall cost me about ten dollars just to look at. The centerpiece of the room, however, was the giant, mahogany desk that dominated everything. It was a piece of furniture that you could land an aircraft on, and it left no question that the man behind it was in charge. That man was Ace Thorndike.

There were five of them all together, not counting the muscle behind me. They all wore expensive suits, fancy shoes, and the kind of haircuts that I was dying to make fun of. And none of those things disguised the fact that each man in the room would have snuffed out a human life with the same amount of thought they gave to drinking their morning coffee.

"Mr. Doyle?" asked the man at the center of the room. It occurred to me that the books that lined the shelves might just be for show. I told Ace my real name and the boys behind the desk reacted to it like it was a punch line to a dirty joke.

"I've heard of you," said Ace, an obscene grin crossing his face. "You're that P.I. who works for food." The trained monkeys behind him all laughed. I had to chuckle a little myself.

"Judging from that gut hanging over your expensive belt, you don't miss too many meals yourself, Ace."

I noticed that I was now the only one in the room wearing a grin, and it didn't seem like a healthy thing to do. One of Ace's men, a short guy in pinstripes on Ace's left, sprinted towards me, his hand digging deep into his jacket. Ace held up a hand and the gunsel stopped dead in his tracks, but the move only helped reinforce the math for me. There were five guns in the room to my one, and that was assuming that Ace himself wasn't packing, which is always a fatal assumption.

"My associate tells me that you are here because you have some information on my... vacation last year," said Ace, with the practiced civility of someone discussing a regatta instead of murder.

"I do seem to recall something to that effect," I said, wearing what I hoped was my best poker face. The stakes were high, and if I misplayed this hand, it might just be...well, aces.

"And what is it that you think you know?"

"I know the whole dirty business about Niles the Nose. I know where, when, and who helped him take a midnight ocean swim and I can prove it." I let that hang in the air, the thunderous quiet more nerve-wracking than the sound of a cocking trigger. "But I don't have to know anything. Not if you could find your way to doing me a small favor."

Thorndike mulled this over as if he were chewing on a tough steak before he answered. "It's a bit early in our relationship to be asking for favors, ain't it? Besides, what's to keep me from making sure that you never speak of anything ever again?"

"What's keeping you is that, contrary to belief, I'm not so stupid as to walk around with the goods on me. If anything happens to me, then the right people will know all about your business. People who aren't in your pocket."

Thorndike closed his eyes for a moment and seemed to reflect on the absurdity that certain individuals existed that were not in his pocket. As he reflected, the muscle behind him remained motionless, even pinstripes, like dogs waiting for the attack order. That didn't stop the kid from trying to bore a hole in my head through sheer willpower. In contrast, Ace maintained the serenity of a Buddhist priest. He slowly opened his eyes and picked up the crystal tumbler on his desk. It held a few fingers of expensive liquid, and Thorndike gazed into the booze as if it held my future, which in a sense it did. He knocked back the glass, draining the alcohol, and turned his attention to me.

"What exactly is this 'favor' that you want?" The tone of his voice conveyed the fact that Ace Thorndike didn't make his way in the world by granting favors, and this was not a practice that he would find habit-forming.

"I want you to leave Hughie Cranski alone," I told Ace.

"Who?"

I sighed, not wanting to actually say the words out loud.

"I want you to forget about Hugh W. Cranston." The blank looks spread though the gallery. "He's that scrawny little pulp writer that lives on the East Side who thinks he's the second coming of Edward R. Murrow."

The silence held in the room for almost two seconds, before it erupted into thunderous, boisterous laughter.

"Are you serious?" asked Ace, once he was able to regain the power of speech. The guys behind him, pinstripes included, were doubled over with laughter.

"Do you hear that?" Ace called over his shoulder. "Tough guy here don't want us to lean on the comic book man." Once again laughter ensued, and I was the straight man in a vaudeville routine.

"I take it that 'Li'l Abner' is still fair game, right boss?" More hilarity ensued, and I found myself wishing for that bullet to come sooner rather than later.

"Think of him what you will, but he's looking into whatever you've got going on Channel Street. I'll talk him out of this, but I want your word that he'll be healthy while I do."

The laughter died as the goons looked over at their boss. Pinstripes bent forward and whispered into Ace's ear.

"Boss, Channel Street?"

Ace Thorndike stood and offered me his hand.

"I think we have a deal," he said, and we shook. The goons behind him stood and watched as if a miracle had taken place. One had, but not in the way I thought. Ace held onto my hand.

"I was going to tell Alberto here to cut you up and feed you to the fish, but this is priceless."

"How do you mean?" I asked, the brief warmth of hope I felt in my chest vanished, replaced by the more common feeling of dread.

"I'll let the kid be, and I expect to never hear the name 'Niles the Nose' for the rest of my life."

"And me?" I asked, my voice breaking like a fourteen year old's.

"You?" he said, letting go of my hand and throwing his arms wide open. A smile spread out over the mobster's face, and he looked as lethal as a toddler. "Boys, do you know what I do on Channel Street every Thursday morning before I come to the office?" he asked. The goons exchanged quizzical glances but kept silent.

"I pick up my laundry!"

The laughter from before was nothing compared to the guffaws that rained down as Ace waved me away. Ace laughed that he was going to have to share this with Boom Boom Bianchi on the East Side.

"Priceless," he said in way of farewell. "Simply priceless."

I made my way back to the elevator and rode down with the monolith who worked the lever. I even heard chuckles come from somewhere down in his dark, tiny little soul.

"Laundry," he muttered. "That's a good one."

Hughie was in the clear with City Hall. No one from Ace Thorndike's mob would harm a hair on the kid's head.

I, however, couldn't wait to kill him.

"Hughie, you are one dead son of a..." I said as I threw open his apartment door. I was immediately greeted by the business end of two gun barrels introducing themselves. In my experience, I've found that the only sensible thing to do in these situations is to remain very still and try not to have an accident. I mentally patted myself on the back for my success. The palookas with the hardware spun me around and pressed my face into the back of Hughie's door. Hands frisked me, relieving me of my favorite pistol, my wallet, and the slight shreds of dignity that I still possessed.

"Why, this isn't mom's apartment?" I stuttered. "I must have made some silly mistake."

"Button it, gumshoe," said the man with a gun in my back. He grabbed my shoulder and tugged me around, showing me the faces of the men who were leading this dance. Both men wore military hair-cuts, dark suits, and very little personality. They flashed badges at me, but their whole demeanor already spelled out who they were.

Feds.

"What business do you have with Hugh W. Cranston," asked flat top, his gun still getting acquainted with my belly.

"We're old pals," I said. "We meet once a week for crocheting."

"Agent Cranston isn't available for crocheting anymore, funny guy," said the other flat top, tossing my wallet back to me and leaving my gun on the table behind him. "He's helping out Uncle Sam regarding important business on criminal activity in the city and knitting isn't on the schedule"

I looked around Hughie's apartment and found that most of his belongings were boxed up or gone, and the drawers in his dresser that held his clothes were open and empty.

"What have you done with Hughie," I asked, before the monkey-wrench that the Feds had tossed into my brain caused my head to explode.

"Wait! Did you say 'Agent Cranston'?"

The two Feds exchanged looks and then fixed their cold stare on me.

"No, we didn't," senior flat top said as they each picked up a box and holstered their guns. They walked to the door and started to leave, neither smiling nor turning away from me as they did. "No one mentioned Hugh Cranston, and you never heard of him. Do we make ourselves clear, gumshoe?"

"Right," I said. "Uncle Sam knows best." I shot them a quick salute as they sent a couple sneers my way and shut the door behind them, leaving me in a disheveled apartment and a befuddled state of mind.

I wandered into the kitchen, hoping that the Feds left the booze, and caught the only break that I'd had in the last ten thousand years. I filled a dirty tumbler, drained it, and filled it up once more. On the stove, the remnants of Ma Cranski's Mulligan Stew bubbled away, and it smelled just as good as before. I found a bowl, took out a spoon, and turned off the stove.

I sat down on the sofa and took care of the booze, which seemed the more pressing matter, before I finished the stew. I felt better not being the only stooge falling for Hughie Cranski's wild tales, but it worried me a bit that the other stooge was my government. I shook my head, which I would do for the rest of my life when Agent Hugh W. Cranston crossed my mind, and told myself that Hughie was probably very happy with his government-issue badge and gun.

I only hoped he didn't shoot himself on the first day at work.

# Ma Cranski's Mulligan Stew

¼ cup of all-purpose flour

1 teaspoon pepper

1 pound lamb stew meat, cubed

1 tablespoon vegetable oil

2 ½ cups of beef broth

1 cup water

2 bay leaves

2 cloves garlic

½ teaspoon dried oregano

½ teaspoon dried basil

½ teaspoon dried dill

3 carrots, cut into 1-inch slices

3 potatoes, peeled and cubed

2 celery stalks, peeled and diced

1 onion, roughly chopped

1 table cornstarch

1 tablespoon minced fresh parsley

- In a large bowl, toss the lamb and bounce it around for a while with the flour, until well-coated. Add the oil to a Dutch oven and brown the lamb.

- Add the broth, water, and spices. Simmer the meat until it is tender, about an hour and a half. Toss in the carrots, potatoes, celery, and onion and cover, simmering the whole megillah for about 45 more minutes, or until the veggies are tender.

- In a spare bowl, take the cornstarch and combine it with about two tablespoons of the stew broth. Mix it well and pour it back into the stew, stirring the whole mess up.

- Bring the stew up to a boil, remove it from the heat, and take out the bay leaf. Let it sit for about five minutes, dole it out in a bowl, and serve with the parsley.

Serves 4-6 G-Men

# THE CASE OF THE ABSENT EXHIBIT
*When the Ghanouj hits the fan*

There's something a little off-putting about the Museum of Natural History. I can't seem to put my finger on it. Perhaps it's the gryphon statues at the front gate, or maybe the fact that they keep the lights so dim that it looks as if the stuffed bears have a glint of hunger in their eyes. Maybe it's the smell of old mummy in the joint, it doesn't make any difference. All I know is that I don't care for the place. When I got a call from Patterson March, an old army crony, to drop by ASAP and help him out, I wasn't too keen for a number of reasons. March was a dandy of sorts, one I never really cared for, but when someone you served with asks a favor, you do it, personality or lack of one be damned. I'd just have to breathe through my mouth for a while.

The museum was all abuzz with activity, in contrast to the stoic exterior of the place. From what I gathered from the posters and banners strung over the dinosaur bones in the main hall, they were premièring a Middle Eastern find of no small significance that night. King Whatizface the All-Powerful from the Sacred Valley of Wherever, I supposed. From the white coats, cleaners, construction men and caterers running around the joint, it looked to me as if old kingie was still in charge. I looked around for March, hoping I could recognize the old bloke after all this time, when one of the guards came over and put a heavy hand on my shoulder.

"The museum is closed," he said, in the same tone you reserved for unwanted solicitors who knocked on your door to ask about your religious affiliations.

"Careful peaches," I told the tall watchman as he gave me a firm but clear shove towards the gryphons out front. "That's my gun shoulder you got your mitts on."

This gave Bluto some pause, and before he could regale me with more stunning conversation, I heard my name called from inside the Egyptian tomb to my left.

Lesser men would have run in terror.

"Patterson March?" I asked, directing my attention into the darkness. Slowly a figure emerged from the pitch, and much to my surprise, Patterson March hadn't changed a bit in years.

March had the lean, athletic build of a tennis player, and the healthy complexion of a man who worked out, ate right, and spent plenty of time outdoors. I resisted the urge to pistol whip him and stuck out my hand. His smile wavered for a second. I suppose the internal debate raged as how to respond when the help want to shake hands. He once again flashed the pearly whites and took my offered mitt. He gave it a few pumps and I managed to get my heart rate down before we spoke.

"Dashed good to see you again, old boy," said March in an affected English accent. From what I remembered of the man, he was born and raised in Flatbush, but perhaps that had changed over the years.

"You asked me to stop by, but you weren't exactly clear to as to what you needed."

March looked over his shoulder before speaking, to the security guard who was about to give me the bum's rush a moment earlier. With a raise of March's eyebrow the guard flat-footed it back to his post, and March and I retired to the smaller hall, away from the hustle and bustle at the main exhibit.

"I'm told," March whispered, "that you are a detective."

"I'm a detective for hire," I replied, with an emphasis on hire. If March heard the emphasis, he did a good job of not showing it.

"We here at the Museum Society are in a bit of a jam, old boy, and we could use someone of your….."

"Expertise?" I suggested.

"Quite," dismissed March. He walked over to the main hall and expected me to follow, as if I were his underling. It bothered me that I followed.

"Three months ago Professor Martin Plath made the discovery of a lifetime in Egypt," Marsh told me, strolling toward the glass display cases.

"A kosher deli?"

"An intact king's tomb!" snapped Marsh. "Plath made the extremely rare discovery of a tomb untouched by looters. The crypt overflowed with riches, jewels, artifacts…."

"Mummies," I sighed, looking around at the wrapped cadavers. "Lots and lots of mummies."

"Exactly! And each of them worth a king's ransom!" I looked over at the dead bodies wrapped like Christmas presents and wondered which one was the king. I doubted the distinction did him much good now.

"And old Professor Plath got King Whatizwhosits…"

"Cheoptu," snapped March. It's always tough when the help is dim-witted. "King Cheoptu of the third dynasty."

"Fine," I said. "So Plath digs up old man Cheoptu and finds his savings account. How did you end up with the goods only a few months later?"

"Professor Plath was an employee of the Museum, and an employee of mine. We took over custody of the find as soon as news of the discovery reached us and arranged for transfer to the museum."

"And Professor Plath?"

"The unfortunate Professor fell victim to the hydrogen sulfide gas that escaped from the tomb upon opening. Tragic, just tragic. The professor's assistant obtained the proper permits and we were fortunate enough to have the artifacts transported post-haste."

I read between the lines close enough to substitute "hydrogen sulfide" for a blade in the back, "assistant" for paid cut-throat, and "permits" for bribery. Professor Plath never stood a chance.

"Well, that's a lovely tale, but what's it got to do with me?"

March again looked over his shoulder and lowered his voice. "The museum has spared no expense in making this the most publicized event of the year. Anyone who is anyone will be at the opening tonight, and everything must go seamlessly."

"Well, March, it looks like you have all the seams accounted for," I said as I watched the caterers put the finishing touches on the spread. Guys like me don't get a chance to partake of canapés and caviar, so I was hoping to stick around for a while.

"Not quite," said March as he stepped closer and spoke in a hushed whisper. "The Dagger of Cheoptu is missing."

"And I'm guessing that the Dagger of Cheoptu isn't exactly a knife of the Swiss variety…?"

"The Dagger of Cheoptu," said March with an indulgent sigh, "is a priceless artifact that is the crown jewel of this exhibit." I would have thought that the crown jewel would have been an actual crown jewel, but I wasn't the archeologist here.

"So what does the dingus look like?"

"The 'dingus' is a gold dagger approximately twelve inches long with a wavy blade, and three large rubies imbedded in its handle."

"Could you use the thing as a weapon?" I asked, going to the places my mind usually took me.

"Good heavens no!" gasped March." Despite the fact that the dagger is made of very malleable metal, it is worth more than some of the lives in this very room!" I had no doubt that mine was one of the lives it was worth more than and his was one of the exceptions. It was that kind of thinking that made March so popular with his men during our army days.

"All right, when did you notice the dagger was missing?" I asked.

"I noticed it was missing when I made my final inspection this morning. We will be opening the exhibit at six o'clock this evening. The dagger was there last night and this morning as well. I've been just about bloody sleeping in this place since the artifacts arrived." He said this as if it explained his surly disposition, but the same smooth operator that ran the Museum of Natural History today was the guy who routinely had me digging trenches during the war. He noticed everything, but cared about damn little.

"Have there been any unusual visitors to the museum this morning?" I asked.

"Just the usual faces," he said. "The handymen who assemble the displays, the cleaning staff, the caterers, and Professor Trainer, the archeologist who took over after Plath's unfortunate demise."

"And has anyone left the museum?"

"No one has left the building since I got here this morning. The guards have set up a perimeter, none have been in the room since this morning, and no one goes in or out of this place without my say so." If he expected me to salute, he would be disappointed.

"Well, it looks like you have everything in hand," I said, tipping up the brim of my hat and heading towards the caterers table. "Let me know how everything turns out."

"Not so fast," he said, ever the commanding officer. "I still don't have the bloody thief."

"Didn't you have everyone here frisked?" I asked.

"I did," he said. "And everyone was clean. There is no way that the dagger left his room."

"Well, then, what could we possibly have to worry about?" I said as I made my way to the display cases. "Maybe we should just check the silverware drawer."

I poked my way through the display area, carefully focusing on the glass case that once held the Dagger of Cheoptu. I noticed the red velvet pillow still bore the faint outline of the blade. I also noticed that the glass case had recently been cleaned of all fingerprints, stray hair, and smudges. Jeeves the butler would be proud.

"I don't suppose you mopped up any bloody footprints this morning?" I asked the young man from the cleaning crew following the construction guys around, preparing for the grand opening. He gave me the same look my butcher gives me when I try to be witty. If there was anything to be learned, it wasn't here.

I put a hand on the top of the display and tilted it back, lifting the edge away. I clenched my jaw and waited for the alarms to go off.

I got nothing.

I looked over at March and saw that his eyes had bugged out like those Argentinian frogs that always look so cute on the cover of National Geographic.

The expression didn't look so cute on March

"How is this possible?" stammered March as he ran towards the display. He gaped and gasped at the display before grabbing one of the construction goons and pulling him towards the exhibit.

"There's no alarm on this display case!" screamed March. The worker looked as if March told him that there were clouds in the sky.

"Don't worry about it, Mac," said the worker calmly. "We'll get it all done before you put anything in there. Just relax." March blinked dumbly at the crew as they went back to work. I backed up a few steps in case March's head exploded.

"So the dagger could have walked out of here at any time during the last day or night?" I asked.

Silence.

"And it might have even made its way out of the museum by now."

More silence.

I thought of mentioning that one of the school children on a field trip might have made off with the dagger, but that might have pushed him over the edge. Instead I made my way over to the buffet line to see how the better half lived. Apparently they lived on shrimp cocktails.

"We is just getting everything put," said the small, gnome-like woman who managed the group of gnome-like women who set up the food. I did my best to keep my eye on the woman who spoke, but as she mixed into the group, I found it hard to tell them apart. So instead, I turned my attention back to the spread that the old women were "just getting put," and was truly impressed. Everything from champagne and foie gras to Crème Brule and chocolate truffles made up this cornucopia of excess. I rolled up my sleeves and dove in while March increased his blood pressure and questioned the staff. Since there was still a bit of mystery in the air I thought I would pace myself. I planned on working my way from asparagus to zeppoles. I only got as far as the letter B before I hit a snag.

"Pardon me," I said to one of the women who were floating about the chow line moving things here and there. "The grub here seems first rate, but do you happen to have a spoon or something for the Baba Ghanouj here?"

The lady sighed and disappeared into the gaggle of women. When she reappeared, she tossed a utensil into the chafing dish without breaking stride. Guessing that I had 'unimportant guest' scribbled on my forehead in indelible ink, I picked up the handle of the utensil and started to load up my dish. It was only after my plate bowed did I notice the utensil I was holding.

"Oh March," I called over my shoulder. From the amount of time March spent yelling at his underlings, you would have thought he'd be out of breath. You would be wrong.

"Don't say another word," barked March, turning his wrath to me. "If you were half the detective you're supposed yourself to be, you would have been able to turn up some clue to the dagger's whereabouts."

"But I think…."

"No, I don't believe that you do," snapped March. "Consider yourself fired. I'll expect you off the grounds in the next five minutes."

March turned on his heel and sped off into one of the smaller galleries in search of someone else's life in which to spread a little sunshine. Since I was not only fired, but never hired in the first place, I loaded up my plate for a nice long lunch at home. Before I left, I wiped the eggplant from the Dagger of Cheoptu and left it neatly in the bussing tray.

# BABA GHANOUJ

2 1-pound eggplants, halved lengthwise

1/4 cup olive oil

1/4 cup tahini (sesame paste)

3 tablespoons fresh lemon juice

½ teaspoon of cracked black pepper

½ teaspoon salt

1 garlic clove, chopped

Pita bread wedges

- Crank up the heat in the oven to about 375 degrees F and slice the eggplant in half while you wait for the oven to do its thing. Put the halves face-down on a baking sheet and throw it in the oven for about 45 minutes, or until the fight is gone from them. Using a spoon, scoop out the guts of the eggplants and sweat them out in a strainer, until they've lost most of their liquid.

- Throw the eggplant guts into a processor and add the olive oil, tahini, lemon juice, salt, black pepper, and garlic. Give it a spin and serve it up with the pita bread.

Suitable for any museum heist.

# The Big Shoulders
## A Special Agent Hugh W. Cranston Adventure

I walked past the stone lions that stood guard over Chicago's Federal building, giving the boys a snappy salute as I did so. I had spent the last three weeks in Mr. Hoover's employ as a recent graduate of the FBI training academy, and felt it was my duty to start each day off right by giving the lads a hearty good morning from Hugh W. Cranston.

The 'W' stood for patriotic!

I made short work of my first assignment of the morning by wearing out a little of the old shoe leather. As the newest agent in the Chicago office, I had to start on the bottom rung of the investigation ladder but, a little elbow grease and my nose to the magnifying glass, and I had already earned the trust of the Bureau Chief, Special Agent Stanton. My only concern thus far was that my meteoric rise might generate the envy of my fellow agents, but such is the life of a civil servant.

I had heard the term 'rookie' bandied about behind my back at the water cooler, but I didn't consider myself a rookie as such. While it was true that I was a recent graduate, since I had gone through the academy twice I thought of myself as a seasoned veteran. Another factor in my favor was that I had opened over forty cases in my short time in the Chicago office, more than any other agent in Bureau history, and had doubled the workload of every agent in the office. I told Special Agent Stanton that there was no need to thank me, that the work was reward enough, but he insisted that I be rewarded by running a special assignment this morning, taking me away from the office.

I threw open the front door, fresh from this morning's success. I heard the odd sigh and grumble escape my fellow agents. I kept my business-like expression, but inside I sympathized. It's hard when you've been toiling away for years in anonymity only to see the spotlight fall on another.

I marched confidently into Special Agent Stanton's office and dropped the package onto his desk. Stanton was a bulldog of a man with a crimson facial hue and a bulging vein on his head that indicated coronary distress may be in his future. He was on the phone when I entered and nodded absently to me, waving me away as he rummaged through his desk for a pencil. I headed back to my desk and fed a sheet of typing paper into my trusty Underwood. In the process of completing my mission I had come afoul of a hot dog vendor who had aroused my suspicions, and my case load could use the boost. I started to type but was interrupted before I finished the word 'frankfurter.'

"Hughie!" yelled Special Agent Stanton. The din in the office faded as all eyes fell on me.

"Uh, it's Hugh W. Cranston, boss," I corrected the Special Agent. It is always a gamble to correct a Special Agent of the FBI. "What can I do for you, chief?"

"Does this look like anchovies to you?" asked Stanton, holding up a hunk of Chicago-style, deep-dish pizza fresh from Rossi's Delicatessen. I removed my glasses, took a handkerchief, gave them a quick wipe, and had a gander. To my trained eye, it did not appear to have any anchovies.

"They assured me that your slice had anchovies, chief."

"That was the only thing I asked…," he grumbled, casting an eye towards heaven as he dropped the wedge back into the brown paper sack. "Go back and grab me another slice."

"But Chief, I just started another report on a possible subversive…."

"We don't need another report on the paper boy," sighed Stanton, rubbing his temples slowly. Ever since I had met the Chief he suffered from sudden onset headaches. One of the burdens of the mantle of responsibility, I suppose. "Go get me my slice."

I stood up and pulled on my coat, preparing for my next mission. As I walked to the door, Stanton called after me.

"And take your time."

Rossi's Deli was the neighborhood hot spot for pizza and pasta, and in Chicago, that said something. When my fellow office dwellers took their daily lunchtime constitutional, their olfactory senses led them here, to wait in line for the best deep-dish pizza Chicago ever crafted. Even though lunchtime was almost over, there was still a fifty-foot long line of famished citizenry. I stood in line for Stanton's slice with anchovies, and hoped that they wouldn't run out of pizza before my turn.

The ladies at the counter worked the line with military efficiency, the sandwiches, containers of pasta, and slices of pizza flying through the front door with considerable haste. After a slight wait I found myself at the head of the line. I felt a bit on the peckish side myself and was debating between rigatoni and ravioli, when a voice behind me called out to one of the women in Italian. The woman nodded at him as he tossed a dollar over my shoulder. Before I could say 'pasta fazool' the last slice of deep dish with anchovies was spirited away, placed in a brown sack, and walked out the door in the hands of the man who had cut in front of me.

Rules are the ties which bind society together, so as a patriot, as well as an agent of the FBI, I felt honor-bound to pursue the man, who I'll refer to as Mr. X. No one puts one over on Hugh W. Cranston.

The 'W' stood for vigilant!

I observed Mr. X proceed to his right, away from my office, and I tailed him. He was a tall, thin, athletic man who wore a rather threadbare blue suit. He swung the pizza sack in the devil-may-care fashion of a subversive, whistling a jaunty tune as he did so.

Although I am not what one may consider an expert on modern music, I think it was 'If I Didn't Care' by the Ink Spots. And while I may not have cared, it would come up in my report, so I made note of it.

Mr. X partook of a bit of window-shopping as he strolled. More than once I saw the mysterious stranger stop and gaze into a storefront window to smooth his hair or straighten his tie. Vanity thy name is Subversion!

As per standard FBI protocol, I kept at least a half-block distance between my subject and myself. I continued to tail Mr. X as he made his way down Main Street, and soon the store fronts and offices gave way to apartments and brownstones. We left the commercial area of town behind and headed towards the residential section. I continued to keep the subject in my line of sight, despite twice stopping to kick a stone out of my shoes and to tie my laces.

Mr. X merrily continued his stroll through the afternoon sun. When he reached the alleyway between Bessie Avenue and Montague Street, he darted quickly to his right and disappeared down the alley. I hesitated for a moment before I broke into a sprint. I made it to the mouth of the alleyway in far more time than my physical trainer at the FBI academy would have cared for. Standing there catching my breath, I found the alleyway empty.

The 'W' does not stand for speedy!

I looked down the alley and saw that one side was made up of the large bay doors of the warehouses of Bessie Avenue, and the other side held the back entrances to the cheap apartments that lined Montague. The trail died in this alley, and it was up to good, old-fashioned, All-American ingenuity to bring it back to life.

I looked at the rusty metal doors along the west end of the alley and my trained analytical eyes noticed that all of them were coated with rust and secured with heavy padlocks. If my quarry had disappeared through them, then the racket he generated would have been heard by J. Edgar himself. It made more sense that my mystery man had disappeared through the back entrance of one of the filthy apartment buildings behind, so that's where I decided to begin my investigation.

Figuring that Mr. X wouldn't have had time to get to the far end of the alley, I tried the first door I came to. It was locked and bolted, and I deduced he wouldn't have had time to get through and bolt it after him. At least not with a sack full of greasy deep-dish. It was the same story with the second door, but the third door spelled success. It was unlocked and even had the tell-tale signs of a grease-smeared hand.

I opened the door and found that the rear entrance led to a long hallway with the front door at the opposite end. Next to me was a staircase that led to the second story. On either side of the hallway were three doors, each belonging to a different apartment. Mr. X could have been anywhere, but the best minds of the FBI had placed their faith in me.

Twice, in fact.

I went to the mail slots at the front entrance and looked at the nameplates. There were eight apartments, and out of the eight four were rented by "Misses," one by the superintendent, two by "Misters," and one by an "F. Brown." Since I doubted that most superintendents wore blue suits to fetch their lunch, I ruled him out. I resolved to start on the first floor and work my way up.

"Good afternoon, citizen," I told the man in apartment three, brandishing my credentials. He was a large, hirsute man in a dirty and worn undershirt. "Agent Hugh W. Cranston of the Federal Bureau of

Investigation. I'm looking into a matter of official Bureau business. I'm searching for…"

And then the door slammed.

In my mind I could hear the training agents of the FBI telling me their agents were made of sterner stuff, but clearly the brute in apartment three was not Mr. X, so I made my way upstairs to the next apartment.

I had paused at the door of apartment seven and was rehearsing my opening speech when it flew open, almost knocking me over. A large, beefy individual wearing black slacks and a white shirt backed into the hallway. His sleeves were rolled to his elbows and sweat seemed to exude from every pore.

"Excuse me, good citizen," I said, just as I had rehearsed in my head a moment before. "If you could spare a moment of your time…."

"Hey, buddy," interrupted the man, throwing me off my speech. "How about giving me a hand with this?" The man was in the process of pulling a large, wooden, dust-covered crate into the hallway. His face contorted with effort and his eyebrows knit together, giving them the appearance of a singular, large, angry caterpillar. His disturbing eyebrows caught me off guard and I couldn't come up with a reasonable excuse not to help. With a shrug I attempted to lift one side of the crate, but it was more substantial than one might have thought.

"As I was saying, sir. I'm with the Federal Bureau of…."

"You gotta put your back into it," said the fellow, a tad more testily than I would have liked.

I grunted and swore before the ability to speak left me. I would have questioned the caterpillar fellow further, but between his growls and my breathlessness, any conversation that might have happened died.

"I'll see if I can get old Mrs. Petravich in apartment six to give me a hand. She's only eighty!" spat the man with the prodigious eyebrows. I leaned on the crate to catch my breath and regain my voice. From where I stood, I could see the man's apartment. The condition of the apartment made me wish that I couldn't.

It was quite literally a rat trap. The floor was strewn with dirty clothes, old newspaper, and rumpled sacks from Rossi's Deli. There was also a large Philco radio on his dresser, blaring the exploits of one "Dexter Reilly, Range Detective." Dexter Reilly was my inspiration for becoming an investigator in the first place. I closed my eyes and listened, but the voice of the Range Detective sounded... off somehow.

I entered the apartment while its occupant was downstairs trying to convince the geriatric woman to come up and help him. Inside I listened, and Dexter's voice seemed a tad too tinny and metallic. I've been an expert on all things Range Detective related since I was eight, so I leaned forward to see what might be wrong with the dusty, old Philco. I squinted at the dial and the sheer amount of dust and grime overwhelmed me. I fell into a sneezing fit the likes of which I had seldom experienced and, as I did, a blast of feedback blared out of the radio, startling my sneezes away.

I examined the old, cathedral-style radio closely. On first inspection it seemed to be the real McCoy, but turning it revealed a strange wire snaking around the electrical cord leading to the wall. I had completed the FBI's surveillance course in the top 7/8ths of my class and considered myself quite the expert on wire-tapping. I clapped my hands together loudly and heard more of the feedback blocking out Dexter Reilly's gripping dialogue.

The wire braided along the AC electrical cord was the same color and thickness of the power cord, and blended perfectly, so much so that John Q. Public would never have guessed that their radio was listening back. John Q. Public, however, was not Agent Hugh W. Cranston of the Federal Bureau of Investigation, and did not possess my level of expertise.

The 'W' stood for expert!

Quietly I drew my service revolver and crept outside.

Downstairs the caterpillar fellow continued his attempt to convince Mrs. Petravich in apartment six to come upstairs and help him move a large box. I heard Mrs. Petravich tell him in broken English that her Goulash was simmering. What one had to do with the other I have no idea, but the pair seemed to have reached an impasse. I left them to work out their own solution as I snuck down the hallway to the neighboring apartment, where the wire led. From a crouch, I gently tapped on the door.

"Waddaya want?" called a gruff voice from inside the apartment.

"Girl Scout cookies," I answered.

"We didn't order any girl scout cookies," came the gruff reply.

"Pizza."

"Look," called the voice, growing louder as the door flew open. "We didn't order any pizza, cookies, or Kung Pao chicken! Now take your sorry…"

I never got the chance to hear what exactly I possessed that was so sorry as the man from Rossi's Deli came face-to-face with a well-polished Government Issue service firearm. The man in the threadbare suit fell silent, but he still wore tell-tale bits of Rossi's deep dish on his jacket, and his devil-may-care visage had turned to a chiseled scowl.

Behind the line-cutter were two of his confederates, both of whom were seated around a large recording device. Their jackets were removed and draped over chairs, and they both wore earphones. Both men also wore shoulder holsters and packed guns. Large guns!

"All right, hands up everybody!" I screamed, trying very hard not to scream. I was told in training by an ex-Marine that my voice went too high when I tried to project an air of authority. He said that he was never able to buy it. Luckily he wasn't here.

"Easy, bifocals," said the man in the suit as he slowly raised his hands. "I think that you're making a big mistake here." Behind him the other two men exchanged glances and shrugged.

It occurred to me that perhaps I needed a bigger gun.

"All right, miscreants, you're under arrest! I want you to slowly take out your firearms and place them on the table in front of you." I saw the two men exchange looks of confusion and motioned them to take off their headphones.

"I said you're under arrest," I repeated patiently, keeping my gun trained on the man that appeared to be their leader. He kept his hands up, but he wore an expression that they failed to teach me at the Bureau.

"Is this guy serious?" asked one of the men at the recorder. His partner shrugged and placed his gun on the table.

It appeared that I was going to have to work on my 'presence of authority.'

"You guys know that I'm arresting you, right?" The leader started to speak, but was interrupted by the voice behind me.

"Mrs. Petravich can't leave her kitchen right now. Are you going to help me with this, or what?"

The browed gentleman stood behind me and peered over my shoulder at the scene unfolding. I saw his face turn from anger to surprise to fear in the span of a moment. It was a breath-taking spectrum of colors. I attempted to explain to the citizen that I was busy at the moment, but he suddenly turned on his heels and ran. I was so surprised I nearly dropped my gun.

The men at the listening post quickly grabbed their weapons. Their leader pulled his weapon from his jacket, and accompanied the pistol with a badge. He roared the word "Police" and sprinted after the citizen, shoving me backwards with more force than I should have thought necessary.

"Cover the fire escape!" barked the lead man to the two others as he bolted down the hall. I fished the badge out of my pocket and held it high above my head.

"Wait, a second," I called after them, my gun pointed at no one in particular. "You can't just…"

"Shut the hell up!" growled the lead cop over his shoulder. As the men split up, I felt that I might have been guilty of a small lapse in judgment. I stood near the wooden crate that dominated the upstairs hallway and tried to figure out how to put all this in my report. As I turned a few snappy phrases over in my head, I noticed my shoelace was untied. The prudent thing to do before springing into action would be to tie it, so my course was clear.

The 'W' stood for prudence!

I had bent over to tie the lace when my world came to a sudden and definite crash.

The man with the single eyebrow had fled downstairs and had dawdled in the hallway, trying to devise an escape. Running to the rear entrance, he met the officers as they made their way down the fire escape. Turning towards the front entrance he saw the officer in the blue suit. In a panic he ran back up the stairs at full speed.

He failed to notice me tying my shoelace.

Tripping over me, the Eyebrow Man found himself airborne, flying full-speed into the wooden crate. With a deafening crash the crate smashed to rubble, and knocked the fugitive unconscious in the process.

I turned to find him napping on a bed of freshly-printed twenty-dollar bills, along with the printing plates for the bills and a small press on which to print them. I stood up and dusted myself off as the officers ran up the stairs, just in time to find their suspect being arrested by yours truly.

I read him his rights, and being unconscious, he chose to remain silent.


The officers, as well as the men around the Bureau, seemed to take the news of my promotion rather poorly, but such is the fate of the rising star. I managed to take down a big fish in the Chicago counterfeiting arena, procuring the first of what I'm sure was to be many commendations by the Washington office, and picked up a pizza sauce recipe for an old friend in the process.

The 'W' stood for, on the rare occasion, "Winning!"

# ROSSI'S ALL-AMERICAN PIZZA SAUCE

1 (28-ounce) can of whole peeled tomatoes

1 tablespoon extra-virgin olive oil

1 tablespoon unsalted butter

2 medium cloves garlic, minced

1 teaspoon dried oregano

Pinch red pepper flakes

Kosher salt

2 sprigs of fresh basil

1 medium yellow onion, diced

1 teaspoon sugar

- Run the tomatoes through a food mill or hand blender until they are pureed. It doesn't have to be completely smooth, but your better angels should tell you when. Set the tomatoes aside.

- Combine the butter and oil in a saucepan and heat over medium-low heat until the butter is melted and the oil is well assimilated. Add garlic, oregano, pepper flakes, and a pinch of salt. Practice vigilance and stir frequently, cooking for about 3 minutes. Add the puree, basil, onion, and sugar. Bring to a simmer and reduce the heat to its lowest setting, with bubbles barely breaking the surface. Remember, patience is a virtue.

- Cook for about one hour, or until the sauce is reduced by ½. Season to taste and allow to cool in a covered container in the icebox. Start a report or two while you wait!

Enjoy with pizza dough and toppings!